Hayley grabbed the car keys on the kitchen counter, jumped in her car, and raced over to Bessie's house.

All the lights were on in the house.

Bessie's car was parked in the driveway.

Hayley raced to the door and rang the bell.

No answer.

She rang again.

Still, nothing.

She tried the doorknob.

It was unlocked.

She poked her head inside. "Bessie? It's me, Hayley. You got me a little worried. Are you okay?"

Hayley walked into the kitchen.

There was a bubbling pot of chocolate on the stove. Some of it was spraying onto the kitchen counter, so Hayley shut off the burner.

A cat jumped up on the counter next to her and began purring.

Another was rubbing up against her leg.

"Bessie?"

Hayley left the kitchen and walked into the living room.

More cats. And they were all gathered around a body on the floor.

It was Bessie.

The phone was still in her hand.

She was dead. . . .

Books by Lee Hollis

DEATH OF A KITCHEN DIVA

DEATH OF A COUNTRY FRIED REDNECK

DEATH OF A COUPON CLIPPER

DEATH OF A CHOCOHOLIC

Published by Kensington Publishing Corporation

A Hayley Powell
Food & Cocktails Mystery

DEATH OF A CHOCOHOLIC

LEE HOLLIS

KENSINGTON PUBLISHING CORP.
http://www.kensingtonbooks.com

KENSINGTON BOOKS are published by

Kensington Publishing Corp.
119 West 40th Street
New York, NY 10018

Copyright © 2014 by Rick Copp and Holly Simason

All rights reserved. No part of this book may be reproduced in any form or by any means without the prior written consent of the Publisher, excepting brief quotes used in reviews.

If you purchased this book without a cover, you should be aware that this book is stolen property. It was reported as "unsold and destroyed" to the Publisher and neither the Author nor the Publisher has received any payment for this "stripped book."

All Kensington Titles, Imprints, and Distributed Lines are available at special quantity discounts for bulk purchases for sales promotions, premiums, fund-raising, and educational or institutional use. Special book excerpts or customized printings can also be created to fit specific needs. For details, write or phone the office of the Kensington special sales manager: Kensington Publishing Corp., 119 West 40th Street, New York, NY 10018, attn: Special Sales Department, Phone: 1-800-221-2647.

Kensington and the K logo Reg. U.S. Pat & TM Off.

ISBN-13: 978-0-7582-9449-4
ISBN-10: 0-7582-9449-2
First Kensington Mass Market Edition: January 2014

eISBN-13: 978-0-7582-9450-0
eISBN-10: 0-7582-9450-6
First Kensington Electronic Edition: January 2014

10 9 8 7 6 5 4 3 2 1

Printed in the United States of America

Chapter 1

He was late.

Twenty-four minutes, to be precise.

Hayley knew this was a bad idea. How could she have allowed her friend Liddy to fix her up on a date? With Liddy's own cousin from Bucksport! He didn't even live in Bar Harbor. And how could she have agreed to meet him on Valentine's Day? Who goes on a blind date on Valentine's Day? That's reserved for moony newlyweds who coo and giggle and feed each other mushy, rich desserts with their fingers. Or for tired, old married couples who feel forced to show the world the magic is still there by dining out at a romantic restaurant, even though they would rather be eating in front of the TV while watching *The X Factor* and not having to talk to each other.

She had tried to cancel, but Liddy wouldn't hear of it because she was convinced that what

Hayley needed most right now was to get right back out there and date after her on-again, off-again boyfriend Lex Bansfield recently blew town for Vermont after losing his job.

Hayley checked her watch again.

This was torture.

Even though it was mid-February, there was no snow on the ground. The temperature was a brisk thirty-seven degrees. No ice on the roads. What possible excuse could he have for being this late? The trip from Bucksport to Bar Harbor was only a little over an hour if he took Route 3.

Hayley gulped down the last of her Merlot and tried to signal Michelle, the bartender/waitress at her brother's bar, Drinks Like A Fish, for her check.

She was not going to wait longer than thirty minutes for a blind date to show up. And that was final.

Michelle's back was turned and then she scurried through the swinging doors into the kitchen and didn't see Hayley waving at her.

Hayley actually felt relieved. Now she could firmly tell Liddy that she had given the whole dating thing a try and it just didn't work out. She certainly wasn't too keen on starting a serious relationship.

Especially so soon after Lex.

Lex was a wonderful man, a real stand-up guy, but he was not without his issues, and Hayley just didn't have the energy right now to devote to a man. Her kids had been extremely demanding lately with their various teen dramas and she wanted to focus more on them and her food-and-cocktails column at the *Island Times* newspaper.

Besides, dating was such a brutal endeavor. And she was never especially good at it. On her first date with Lex, she wound up arrested. But that was another story.

Michelle breezed out of the kitchen, and Hayley finally caught her attention. Hayley quickly made a scribbling motion with her finger, indicating she would like to pay for her wine and get the hell out of there, but then she felt a cold chill on her back as the front door swung open and a blast of winter air swept through the bar. She nearly jumped out of her chair as the door banged shut.

Hayley closed her eyes.

Please let it not be him.

Please let it not be him.

"Hayley?"

Hayley took a deep breath and swung her head around, hoping for the best.

"Yes. Walter?"

Walter nodded. He was taller than Hayley had expected. Much taller. In fact, there was a slight pain in her neck as she craned her head up to meet his face. The first thing she noticed was he had a beautiful head of dirty-blond hair. Wavy and thick and a bit shaggy. But then her eyes settled on his face. Nice features, but something was definitely off. Maybe it was the low lighting in the bar, but it looked almost as if his cheeks—no, the whole left side of his face was drooping or slightly deformed. This certainly didn't come across in the photos on his Facebook page, which Hayley had researched before agreeing to meet him.

He shed his winter coat and draped it on the back of the chair and sat down across from Hayley. "I was hoping you wouldn't notice."

Hayley tried acting nonchalant. "Notice what?"

"My face. I had a small cosmetic procedure today, and the doctor warned me this might happen for a day or two until my face settles. My mother begged me to reschedule because with my nasty luck, she knew something like this might scare you off."

Cosmetic procedure?

Mother?

"Is it some kind of medical issue?"

"Oh no. Nothing that dramatic. Just a little face-lift. We're not getting any younger, and you know what they say, 'If you want to sell the used car, you need to keep it looking shiny and new.'"

Hayley had never heard anyone say that.

Face-lift?

"So, is it noticeable?" he asked, a mask of genuine concern on his face.

Or at least half of it.

Hayley leaned forward slightly. "You can hardly tell."

That was a huge lie. He looked a bit like the Batman villain Two-Face: one side of the face normal, the other horribly disfigured.

Michelle stopped by the table. "What can I get you?"

Michelle's eyes nearly popped out of her head at the sight of Walter's misshapen face, but she instantly recovered and smiled, pretending not to be startled.

"Just some coffee. I have to drive back home to Bucksport. And do you have any desserts here? I have a raging sweet tooth."

"Yes, we do," Michelle said, pointing to a plastic bar menu in a metal holder on the table. "I recommend the German chocolate cake."

Michelle winked at Hayley knowingly. Randy had recently decided to serve sandwiches and appetizers and a few desserts at his bar, and the new food menu had been a huge hit with his customers. Hayley helped out by baking a few of her signature desserts for him.

Walter ordered the German chocolate cake, and Michelle scooted back into the kitchen, leaving Hayley with Droopy Face.

"So, Hayley, you're much prettier than your photo. Tell me a little bit about yourself," Walter said, trying to be seductive.

Hayley couldn't take her eyes off his sagging cheek; it was making her uncomfortable. She just wanted to bolt out of there, but she couldn't be rude—and Liddy would never forgive her.

So she just rattled off a litany of bullet points about her life. Born and raised in Bar Harbor. Divorced. Two kids. Food-and-cocktails columnist for the paper. Then she quickly turned the conversation over to him.

Walter relished talking about himself: How he had been a high-school basketball star. How his dashing good looks drew women like flies, but he had very high standards, which explained why he had yet to marry. How he was engaged once, but his mother didn't approve; so the relationship was doomed from the start.

There is that mother again.

Mentioned twice in five minutes!

That was never a good sign.

His cell phone rang, interrupting his incredibly boring life story.

He fished it out of the back pocket of his khaki pants and glanced at it.

"It's my mother. I should take this."

Three times in five minutes.

Half his face lit up as he answered the call.

The other half sagged a bit more.

"Mother, you minx. You know I'm on a date," he said, winking at Hayley.

Hayley forced a smile.

"Yes, she's quite pretty. No, she says you can't notice it. I checked myself in the rearview mirror in the car before I came in and I thought it did look a bit slouchy, so maybe she's just being polite. Oh. Okay."

Walter held out the phone. "She wants to talk to you."

"Excuse me?"

"Mother. She wants to speak with you."

Hayley just sat there, mouth agape for a few seconds, before robotically holding out her hand for the phone and putting it to her ear. "Hello?"

"Hi, Hayley, this is Walter's mother, Mary Beth."

"Hello, Mary Beth."

Michelle delivered the cup of coffee and the German chocolate cake. Hayley watched horrified as Walter scarfed it down, getting smears of the coconut pecan frosting lodged on the side of his sagging face while she listened to his mother on the other end of the phone.

"I told Walter not to meet you so soon after his surgery. I always say you need to put your best foot forward on a first date. Make a good impression. 'Why not give your face a couple of days to settle before meeting Hayley?' That's what I told him, but do you think he listened to me? Of course not! He insisted that from what Liddy told him, you would not be shallow enough to judge him on a little temporary side effect from his procedure."

She was wrong.

Hayley was judging. She felt bad about it, but she just couldn't help herself.

Walter finished off the cake and was now slurping his coffee.

"He's normally quite handsome, Hayley. You're going to have to trust me on that," Mary Beth cooed. "All the women in Bucksport are after my son, but they're just silly girls with no ambitions. I told Walter he needed somebody of substance, someone with a career. Someone creative. I adore cooking. I'm somewhat of an amateur chef myself. And when my niece Liddy mentioned you were a food writer, well, I just knew we had to meet you."

"We"? Did Mary Beth just say "we"?

"Anyway, I would love for you to give him another chance. Try again in a couple of weeks, once his face settles. I'm positive you won't be disappointed."

Hayley nodded, dumbfounded, before realizing Mary Beth couldn't see her through the phone. She cleared her throat. "Um, okay."

It was never going to happen.

"Thank you, Hayley. I cannot wait to meet you. I suspect we'll be fast friends. I hope you like to knit, because I've already told the women in my knitting circle all about you."

"Bye," Hayley said flatly, handing the phone back to Walter, who pressed it to his ear and grinned.

"I hope you didn't embarrass me, Mother."

They chatted a few more seconds and then Walter shut off his phone and stuffed it back into his pants pocket.

Michelle swung by the table. "How did you like the cake?"

"It was a little dry," Walter said huffily. "I think you need a new chef."

Michelle glanced at Hayley, who shook her head. Best not tell him she baked the cake.

Michelle turned back to Walter. "Can I get you anything else?"

"Just the check," Walter demanded.

Michelle tore it off her pad and slapped it down on the table. As she walked away, Hayley noticed Walter checking out her ass.

Seriously?

Walter let the check sit there for a few seconds.

As if he was hoping Hayley was going to reach for it first.

So she did.

Walter raised the palm of his big bony hand to stop her. "No. No. Allow me."

Maybe chivalry wasn't dead in Bucksport.

"You can get it next time," he said.

Yes, it was quite dead.

He reached into the other back pocket of his khakis.

Half his face froze.

He then frantically searched the pockets of his winter coat, which was draped over the back of his chair, before giving Hayley a sheepish grin. "I must have left my wallet in the car. You wait here. I'll go get it."

"No!" Hayley almost screamed as she snatched the check out of his hand and slammed some money down on the table, perhaps a little too hard. She couldn't stand another minute with Droopy Dog. "You can get it next time."

"You really shouldn't have to pay. I mean, Liddy told me your brother owns this place. They should comp you. Kind of rude of him, don't you think?"

Hayley just stared at him.

His sagging face actually fit his personality.

Liddy . . . the mastermind behind this nightmare.

Hayley was going to have to resist the urge to kill her BFF for putting her through this wretched evening.

Especially since she was about to have another dead body on her hands.

Chapter 2

After leaving a very detailed message on Liddy's voice mail explaining how her friend's days as Yenta the Matchmaker were officially over, Hayley drove home. She found her fifteen-year-old son, Dustin, sprawled out on the couch in the living room. He was wearing boxer shorts and a *Family Guy* t-shirt; a Boston Red Sox cap was pulled down so far that it shadowed his eyes. He was snoring softly, with the TV blasting. Hayley picked up the remote from the coffee table and shut off the television. She knelt down and gently shook his shoulder.

"Hey, sleepyhead, time for bed. You have school tomorrow."

Dustin half opened one eye and looked at his mother and then turned his head away into the back of the couch. "No, I want to sleep down here. If I go upstairs, the evil witch will come after me again."

"You were just having a bad dream. Now let's go."

Dustin swiveled his whole body back around to face his mother. "It wasn't a dream. Trust me. She's in a really foul mood and I don't want her biting my head off again."

"Gemma? What's wrong with her?"

Dustin shrugged. "Beats me. I just knocked on her door and asked to borrow some toothpaste and she started screaming at the top of her lungs at me to go away. So if I have bad breath right now, it's totally her fault."

Hayley climbed to her feet and headed for the stairs.

"Seriously. I wouldn't go up there if I were you," Dustin said.

"I'm not afraid of my own daughter."

Hayley started up the steps.

"You say that now," Dustin warned.

When Hayley reached the second floor, she saw Gemma's door open a crack at the end of the hall. The light was still on. Hayley took a deep breath before lightly tapping on the door.

"Gemma, you still up?"

No answer.

"Gemma?"

At least she wasn't screaming.

Hayley pushed the door open a bit more until she got a view of Gemma's bed. The covers were bunched up at the end of the mattress and Gemma sat up against the headboard in flowery shorts and a pink tank top. Earbuds were planted in her ears, and she was watching something on her iPad. Hayley instantly noticed Gemma's watery eyes. It looked as if she either had a cold or had been crying.

Hayley stepped into the room; Gemma finally looked up and noticed her. Instead of acknowledging her mom, Gemma went back to staring at her iPad.

"Is everything okay?" Hayley asked.

Nothing.

"Gemma, I'm talking to you," Hayley said, taking a step closer to the bed.

Gemma yanked one earbud out and sighed. "What? I'm trying to watch *The Vampire Diaries.*"

"Your brother said you were pretty moody with him earlier."

"Big deal. He was bothering me. And when did he get to be such a tattletale?"

"You want to talk about it?"

"No."

"Talking about it always makes you feel better."

"I am not interested in a therapy session. Especially with my mother. So, can we please drop it?"

Hayley saw the headlights from a car pull into the driveway outside Gemma's bedroom window. Who could be stopping by this time of night? The only person she could think of was Liddy.

If Liddy knew what was good for her, she was definitely here to beg for forgiveness.

Hayley turned back to Gemma, who had already shoved her earbud back into her ear and was staring at the screen of her iPad. She sniffed, as if she was fighting back tears. She refused to make any more eye contact with her mother.

Hayley decided to let it go.

For now.

Sometimes the odds of getting a teenager to talk were about as high as winning the million-dollar lotto. Which Hayley still tried doing on occasion, given how she was constantly drowning in bills. So it was probably best to give her daughter some space and try approaching her again in the morning.

As Hayley walked back down the stairs, she heard the door to the kitchen open and a voice call to her, "Don't kill me for showing up so late."

Hayley smiled.

It was her brother, Randy.

She rounded the corner and saw him standing in the kitchen, wearing sweats and a t-shirt, furry slippers and a winter coat thrown over his shoulders. He was holding a big square box in his hand, and there was a brown bath towel covering it.

"How'd your date go?" he asked.

"Don't ask. What's that?"

"Please don't be mad," Randy said.

Whenever her brother said, "Please don't be mad," it always meant bad news for Hayley.

"What, Randy? What is it?"

"I was going to wait and come over in the morning, but I was afraid Sergio would kick me out before then, so I had to take care of it tonight."

"Take care of what? What are you talking about?"

Dustin strolled down the hall into the kitchen from the living room and opened the refrigerator to grab a carton of milk. "Hey, Uncle Randy, what did you bring us?"

Randy slowly pulled the brown bath towel off the box.

Dear God, no.

It wasn't a box.

It was a pet carrier.

And inside was a big, fat Persian Blue cat. He growled menacingly. His yellow eyes fixated on Hayley like some caged violent criminal behind bars who vowed to wreak havoc if he ever broke out.

It was Blueberry.

Hayley knew this animal all too well. He was the pet of a local in town, and Hayley agreed to look after the cat briefly while the owner was incapacitated. It was during a very stressful time when Hayley's furnace was busted and she was staying with Randy. Blueberry relished terrorizing everyone in the house, and left behind a devastating path of destruction.

Unfortunately, Blueberry's owner had recently

left town unexpectedly; and Blueberry was now homeless, but that was a whole other story.

Right now, the question was what was this devil cat doing in her kitchen?

"I know what you're thinking," Randy said. The words tumbled out of his mouth at such a speed Hayley could barely understand him. "Why would I ever allow this horrible creature who hates every other living thing to set one paw back inside my house, especially after he peed on every rug and upholstered piece of furniture I own?"

"Yes, that's exactly what I'm thinking," Hayley said, crossing her arms.

"Because I've always been a sucker for a sob story, you know that, and when I heard from Michelle, who volunteers part-time at the animal shelter, that they were planning to put him down because nobody wanted to adopt him given his, well, diabolical nature, I just couldn't stand by and let them do it. I heard myself saying the words 'I'll take him' and yet it was like I was outside my body watching myself sign the papers and walk out of the shelter with the carrier. It was so surreal. Like it was happening to someone else.

"But then I got home and I let him out of the carrier, and it hit me like a two-by-four. Why this was always going to be a terrible mistake. He started tearing up the place, and peeing every-where, and threw up a hairball in Sergio's slipper."

Sergio.

Randy's partner.

And the town's police chief.

"When Sergio went to grab him, Blueberry scratched the hell out of his hand. Now my relationship is teetering on the edge. Sergio is furious I brought him home without checking with him first. He doesn't even like cats. He's allergic. How was I to know? After all, he was in Brazil the last time Blueberry was around. He never came in contact with him."

"You've been living with the man for ten years. You didn't know he was allergic to cats?"

Randy shook his head, a panicked look on his face. "What am I going to do?"

"Take him back to the shelter," Hayley said firmly.

"I know he's a little high maintenance, but is that reason enough to kill him?" Randy asked.

"Well, what other choice do you have?"

"Well, I was hoping you might—"

"No! Don't even go there."

"Just until we can find him a permanent home."

"Absolutely not. I don't think Leroy's heart could take it."

Leroy was Hayley's white Shih Tzu, with a pronounced underbite. He was also the number one victim of Blueberry's terrorist activities. The poor dog cowered in fear at the mere thought of this angry, furry blue butterball.

"Why is he looking at me funny?" Dustin asked, staring at Blueberry, whose yellow eyes narrowed as he glared from inside the metal carrier.

"He's trying to suck out your spirit," Hayley said. "It's one of his wicked powers."

"He's kind of freaking me out. I'm going to go hide in my room. Night, Uncle Randy," Dustin said, putting the milk back in the fridge, then pounding down the hall and up the stairs.

"Night, buddy," Randy said, before turning back to Hayley. "Blueberry's not that bad."

"No, he's not that bad—now that he's in my house and not yours. You know I'm a bleeding heart, Randy, just like you, and I'm really, really mad at you for taking advantage of that."

"I will pay for all expenses—food, shots, medicine, anything he needs."

"And you'll reimburse me for anything in my house that he might destroy?"

"Yes. Absolutely. And I will find him a place to live. I promise. Just give me a week. Maybe two. But no more than three. It's been pretty busy lately at the bar."

"Why do I have the feeling I'm going to regret this?"

Leroy, who had been sleeping in the recliner in the living room, ambled into the kitchen. His little tail had been wagging at the sound of Hayley's and Randy's voices, but he stopped in his tracks at the familiar sight of the pet carrier. His eyes went wide in abject horror as Randy unlatched the door to the carrier and pulled it open.

Blueberry sauntered out calmly, swishing his tail around, taking in his surroundings.

Leroy stood his ground, but he kept glancing at Hayley, like he was begging to know what on earth would possess her to allow this dangerous presence onto his home turf.

Blueberry calmly marched forward, stopping less than an inch from Leroy's face. He sniffed Leroy, and his whiskers tickled the little dog's nose.

For a moment, it looked as if Blueberry might be calling a truce.

Leroy bought it.

He sniffed back.

But then the devil cat flicked open his claws and swiped them across Leroy's face, drawing a tiny bit of blood above the nose.

Instead of retreating, Leroy began snapping at Blueberry with his bared teeth. Hayley and Randy raced to intervene and pulled the two prize-fighter pets apart.

Let the games begin.

Chapter 3

"Six days and seven nights in Isla Mujeres," Bruce Linney said, waving the brochure in front of his boss *Island Times* editor in chief Sal Moretti's face. "You know what 'Isla Mujeres' means, don't you, Sal?"

"I never took Spanish in high school," Sal grumbled as he poured himself a cup of coffee.

"Island of Women," Bruce said, winking, before unfolding the brochure and holding it up for Sal to see. "And my buddies who've been there before told me it's definitely not false advertising!"

Hayley kept her eyes on her computer, not at all anxious to join the conversation. She was already jealous that crime reporter Bruce was able to afford a first-class two-week Mexican vacation and she was struggling to pay her winter heating bill.

"Take a look at the villa we've rented. You

wouldn't believe how cheap it was, especially since I'm pooling with my fraternity brothers."

"Nice," Sal said, before sucking down his coffee and trying to make a quick escape to his office in the back of the *Island Times* building.

No such luck.

"Just think. This time Saturday I'll be sipping a cocktail on the deck of this incredible rental house, watching the sun set over the ocean, a hot Mexican chick in a tube top and a flowery sarong nestled in my lap, slowly licking the salt off my face from the margarita glass, while I'm high-fiving my college buddies."

"Oh, dear God, Sal, make him stop," Hayley moaned, unable to hold her tongue anymore.

"She's right," Sal said. "Don't rub it in."

"Sorry," Bruce said, smirking. "I'm sure you'll have a nice weekend too, Hayley. Maybe you can drive up to the Bangor Mall and buy a new vacuum or something."

"If you ever saw the inside of my house, Bruce, you'd know I rarely vacuum," Hayley said, half joking.

Actually, she wasn't joking at all. She couldn't afford to hire a maid and she was usually too tired from work and parenting to get much housework done on the weekends.

"Hayley isn't going to have time to take any joy rides to Bangor, Bruce. She's going to be way too busy writing both columns while you're gone," Sal said, pouring what was left in the coffee pot into his cup and then slurping it down in one gulp.

"What do you mean *both* columns?" Bruce asked.

"I thought Hayley could fill in for you while you're gone," Sal said.

Bruce looked at Sal and then at Hayley, his mouth agape, before suddenly bursting into a fit of giggles. "Good one, Sal. You almost had me."

"I'm serious," Sal said.

"No, you're not," Bruce said, still laughing.

"Yes, I am. I really am."

Bruce suddenly stopped laughing. "You're going to let *Hayley* write my 'Police Beat' column?"

Sal nodded.

"Well, that's about the dumbest idea I've ever heard."

"You might want to rephrase that, since it was *my* idea," Sal warned. "I can go back to my office and dig up your vacation days request and stamp a big fat 'Denied' on it if you keep pissing me off."

"It's just . . . I mean, I thought my column would go on hiatus while I was on vacation."

"Oh, so you think crime in Bar Harbor is just going to stop while you fly off to Mexico?" Sal snorted. He glanced over at Hayley, who was still in shock over the sudden doubling up of her workload.

"But why Hayley? I mean, no offense, but she is supremely *un*qualified."

"Wow. How could I ever take offense to that,

you silver-tongued devil?" Hayley said, rolling her eyes.

"Let's be honest, Sal. She's never had any real writing experience. I have a journalism degree from Boston University. Hayley majored in Jack Daniel's shots at the University of Maine at Farmington before dropping out after freshman year for lack of attendance. And let's face it, you pay her to dole out all these recipes to our readers and she's never taken one cooking class."

"You do realize I'm sitting right here," Hayley said.

"And she gets more fan letters in a week than you do in a year," Sal said.

That shut up Bruce.

For about a second.

He opened his mouth to speak again.

Sal cut him off, delivering the final blow. "And if you really want to be honest, just by being annoyingly nosy, she's also solved more local crimes in the past couple of years than you have."

Hayley wanted to cheer Sal for so valiantly coming to her defense.

But she could've done without him calling her "annoying."

And "nosy."

Bruce's face flushed with anger.

He was speechless.

And that was about as rare as a tornado in Maine.

Bruce shook his head, staring at Hayley in utter

disbelief, before averting his eyes back to Sal, as if waiting for the editor to burst out laughing and tell him it was all just a sick joke.

But Sal held his ground.

His sour puss expression never changed.

Finally accepting defeat, Bruce marched through the door into the back bull pen, retreating into his office, and slamming the door behind him.

There was a deafening silence.

Hayley's mind was racing. How on earth would she ever be able to write two columns at once? She was already inundated with her office manager duties aside from her own food-and-cocktails columns. Not to mention parenting two rambunctious teenagers, one of whom was in the midst of an undisclosed crisis. She knew she had to speak up now or be stuck with an overwhelming workload.

"Sal, I appreciate the opportunity to fill in for Bruce, but I don't see how I can manage—"

"I'll double your salary for the next two weeks until Bruce gets back."

"I won't let you down, boss," Hayley blurted out.

Suddenly the idea of writing two columns didn't seem so daunting.

Island Food & Spirits
by
Hayley Powell

The other night, after I finished washing the dishes from dinner, I glanced at the clock and realized that it was only seven o'clock. I still had time to whip up one of my famous German chocolate cakes that my brother, Randy, had recently started selling at his bar. The more cakes I made and he sold, the more extra spending money I would have in my pocket for the slots in Bangor. So let the cake baking begin!

As I gathered together my ingredients on the kitchen counter, my mind wandered back a few years ago to when the kids were smaller and more rambunctious and how hectic the nights always were before and after dinner. Inevitably, I would forget to check their backpacks to see if there were any notes or other important information. Asking the kids if there was something I needed to sign or know about always proved fruitless because once they finished eating, their eyes would be glued to the television and they completely tuned me out.

I should have been more diligent after learning my lesson at a recent parent-teacher conference. I was approached by two parents (who shall remain nameless, but you know the type—the ones who fancy themselves above all others and appoint themselves in charge of every event). Anyway, the Super Moms cornered me in the hallway and quietly asked me if everything was all right at home, since my absence from the monthly PTA meetings hadn't gone unnoticed. They also added that they were shocked that I wasn't even contributing to the classroom bake sale fund-raisers. After exchanging a look of judgment, they turned on their pointy high heels and clicked down the hallway, looking like twin Barbie dolls. I just stood there with my mouth hanging open (once again).

That night when I got home, I tore through my kids' backpacks and pulled out every scrap of paper. Oh, what a mess! But I found schedules for the meetings, dates for bake sales, book sales, and crumpled-up announcements of every other upcoming scheduled event for the whole semester. Then I searched the house for my organizer calendar, which I had purchased before the school year began just to avoid all of this drama (although I did note to myself that I hadn't even taken it out of the wrapper yet).

After frantically filling in all of the dates for every upcoming activity, I must admit I was quite proud of myself. I even managed to attend the next PTA meeting while pretending not to notice a few raised eyebrows as I made my way to an open seat in the front of the classroom.

A few weeks later I was up way too late on a work night, watching a cheesy-but-oh-so-good Lifetime Movie Network thriller about some soap actress with a murderous stalker. Actually, he was better-looking than she was and had six-pack abs. I had to wonder why she was so upset that he was standing outside her bedroom window, but I digress. I turned off the TV and walked into the kitchen to shut off the light, and just happened to glance at the calendar on the fridge. There right in front of me in huge glaring red letters were the words *BAKE SALE*! Oh, my God! And it was tomorrow!

I vowed I was not going to miss this one and have those prissy, perfect mothers talking behind my back; so I ran all over the kitchen, throwing open the cupboards and grabbing the ingredients for my German chocolate cake, which I decided to turn into German chocolate cupcakes. I could just double the recipe so there would be more than enough to sell at the bake sale. I was up until the wee hours of the morning, baking and frosting and packing up my moist cupcakes into three boxes, before finally collapsing into my bed, around 3:00 A.M., and dreaming about that handsome stalker chasing *me* around the house instead of pursuing that whiny soap actress.

When I opened my eyes in the morning, the sun was streaming through the window and the house was unusually quiet. I turned to glance at the clock and sat up in horror! It was 7:45 A.M.! We were late! I leapt out of bed, screaming the kids' names! They groggily pulled on their clothes as I threw together their lunches while trying to come up with an excuse for Sal as to why I was going to be over an hour late for work.

Finally the kids, backpacks, myself, and four dozen cupcakes were packed into the car and we raced off to school. Of course, I had to hear about how it was *my* fault we all overslept because I didn't wake up Gemma and now her perfect-attendance record was going to be ruined. Note to self: *Get the kid her own alarm clock for Christmas*. Once we squealed to a stop in front of the school, I shoved everyone out of the car and then hit the gas and sped off to the office. Luckily, the rest of the day was relatively quiet. Until I got home at five and found Gemma standing in the middle of the kitchen with her hands on her hips, staring daggers at me.

Oh, Lord, I knew that look. It was always followed by an eye roll and a big sigh. Not a good sign. She informed me that *once again* she was the only kid in her class who didn't bring something to sell at the bake sale! What was she talking about? I made four dozen cupcakes! And then it hit me. With all of the confusion that morning, the cupcakes were still sitting in the back of the car, where I had so carefully placed them.

At this point there was only one thing to do. Make a cocktail, grab a cupcake (or two), and sit down and try to figure out how to get rid of four dozen German chocolate cupcakes tomorrow.

Red Velvet Cupcake Cocktail

<u>Ingredients</u>
2 ounces vanilla vodka
1 ounce crème de cacao
1 ounce buttermilk (you'll need it for the next recipe too)
1 tablespoon chocolate sauce
3 drops red food coloring
8 drops of vanilla extract
Ice, as needed
Frosting for the rim of the glass (store bought is fine)

Mix your vodka with the crème de cacao, buttermilk, chocolate sauce, red food coloring, and vanilla extract in a shaker with ice. Strain and pour into a glass rimmed with frosting.

Hayley's German Chocolate Cake

<u>Ingredients</u> (for the cake)
1 (4 ounce) package sweet dark chocolate
½ cup water
2 cups flour
1 teaspoon baking soda
¼ teaspoon salt
1 cup butter, softened
2 cups sugar
4 eggs, separated
1 cup buttermilk
1 teaspoon vanilla extract

<u>Ingredients</u> (for the frosting)
1 (12 ounce can) evaporated milk
1½ cups sugar
¾ cup butter
4 egg yolks, slightly beaten
1½ teaspoons vanilla extract
2⅔ cups coconut
1½ cups chopped pecans

Grease and flour the bottoms of three (9-inch) round cake pans, and line with parchment paper. Melt the chocolate and water in a double boiler. Stir until chocolate is completely melted.

Sift flour, baking soda, and salt; set aside.

Beat butter and sugar in large bowl with electric mixer on medium speed until light and fluffy. Add the egg yolks, one at a time, mixing well after each yolk. Stir in chocolate and vanilla.

Add flour mixture alternately with the buttermilk, beating well after each addition.

Beat egg white with electric mixer on high speed until stiff peaks form. Fold into your batter and pour evenly into prepared pans.

Bake at 350 degrees for 30 minutes or until a toothpick inserted into the center of the cake comes out clean. Immediately run a spatula between the sides of your pan and cake; cool for 30 minutes and remove parchment paper and cool on wire racks.

For the frosting, in a large saucepan add the milk, sugar,

butter, egg yolks, and vanilla, stirring constantly and cook on medium heat 12 minutes or until thickened and golden brown. Remove from heat and stir in coconut and pecans.

Cool to room temperature to a spreading consistency. Then spread the mixture on the tops of the cakes. Stack the three cakes and finish frosting the sides and top.

Chapter 4

Hayley decided to celebrate her temporary windfall by swinging by the Shop 'n Save after work and purchasing three filets mignons for her and the kids for dinner. Gemma especially was a wildly enthusiastic carnivore, so perhaps an expensive piece of meat might help improve her mood.

As usual, the grocery store was packed right after work. Hayley was having trouble maneuvering her grocery cart through the meat and poultry section because of the crowd of shoppers pawing over the ground beef and cuts of steak and boneless, skinless chicken. She thought it best to wait and come back in a few minutes after the traffic jam of metal carts had dispersed.

Hayley veered her cart to the right and steered toward the produce section where she could stock up on some fresh vegetables for a salad and a few rustic potatoes she could bake as a side dish to the steaks. She stopped to tear off a plastic bag from the roll next to the lettuces and perused the washed romaine, when she heard shouting coming from behind her.

Hayley spun around to see who was causing the commotion.

It was Ron Hopkins, the owner of the Shop 'n Save. His face was beet red and his eyes were flaring. He was wagging a finger at someone whose back was to Hayley.

But there was no mistaking who that someone was.

Bessie Winthrop.

Hayley had known Bessie since high school. They were never particularly close but always managed a friendly wave whenever they spotted each other. Bessie was what you might call a local eccentric. She was five feet two inches tall and weighed roughly three hundred pounds. She was fond of bright rainbow-colored blouses and muumuus, which certainly called attention to her if her loud, booming voice failed to do so. There was no volume control on Bessie. Screaming her order while dining at any of the local restaurants always drew irked stares. She had a massive head of hair, which was teased out in all different directions. Everyone in town prayed they wouldn't end up sitting behind her in a movie theater. Bessie lived alone, never married, and had a small tattoo of Garfield, the cartoon cat, on the back of her neck.

Ron finished his tirade and tried to walk away, but Bessie reached out and grabbed his arm with her pudgy fingers. She was clutching a small white box wrapped in pink cellophane that matched the pink parka she was wearing over her multi-colored muumuu. She tried to force the box on Ron. He struggled to free himself from her grip and knocked into her. The cellophane-wrapped box rolled off her bosom and landed on the floor. This just made Bessie even angrier.

She kept an iron viselike grip on Ron's arm and bellowed, "Don't walk away from me! I'm not done talking to you, Ron!"

"Well, I'm done talking to you! Now let go of me!"

She wouldn't. She latched onto his other arm with her free hand, trying to pin him down like a Greco-Roman wrestler. Ron hated to be touched. Just ask his wife, Lenora, who was at the moment filing for divorce and asking for a huge settlement. So the idea of Bessie's hands all over him was more than he could handle.

Ron glanced around, desperate for some kind of intervention. But the only shopper within spitting distance was Tilly McVety, a nurse at the local hospital, who stood frozen in her tracks near the oranges and grapefruits, desperate not to get involved.

That left Hayley.

She dropped a potato back on the pile and pushed her cart over to help rescue Ron.

"Excuse me, Ron, I hate to interrupt you, but the green peppers look a little sad and picked over. When's a new shipment of produce expected to come in?"

Ron looked as if he could cry, he was so grateful. "Tomorrow."

Bessie was so surprised by Hayley's sudden presence that she loosened her grip, allowing Ron to wrench his arm free and quickly step away from her. While doing so, he accidentally stepped on her cellophane-wrapped box with the heel of his shoe and crushed it.

Bessie just stared at the demolished box and the wrinkled cellophane; her eyes welled up with tears.

"Bessie, is everything all right?" Hayley asked.

Bessie spun her head around to Hayley, wiped her snotty nose with her forearm, and nodded curtly before pushing past Ron and out of the store.

Ron was rolling up his shirtsleeve and inspecting his arm. "Look, Hayley, look what she did to me!"

He thrust out his arm, where there were three barely perceptible red marks. "I should have that crazy woman arrested for assault!"

"Ron, calm down and tell me what happened."

Ron reached down and picked up the crushed

box Bessie dropped. "She's a loon, Hayley. She came in here with this box of her homemade chocolates and insisted I carry them in my store. Like she's trying to sell me a Whitman's Sampler or she's from friggin' Godiva! She's insane!"

"It's not such a stretch to think you might carry her product, Ron. You sell Ida Redmond's homemade jams and what about Jackson Mullet, that local artist from Lamoine? I've bought a couple of his greeting cards from this store."

"Yes. Okay. Busted. But Ida's jam is delicious and people love that Mullet guy's cards! Who is going to want to buy chocolates they know Bessie made in her kitchen?"

"I don't understand."

"Oh, Hayley, come on, you're not living in a bubble. You must know about Bessie's living conditions."

All Hayley knew was that Bessie lived in a small two-story house near the end of Ledgelawn Avenue. From the outside it looked perfectly cute and charming.

"She's shacked up with about fifty cats. When my wife, Lenora—excuse me, soon-to-be ex-wife—was trying to make some extra cash selling makeup last year, she stopped by Bessie's house. Bessie insisted she come inside for a cup of coffee, and Lenora said the place was right out of the TV show *Hoarders*. There were filthy cats everywhere and smelly litter boxes right out in the middle of the living room. When Lenora went to take a sip of her coffee, there was white fur floating in it like a friggin' marshmallow."

"I can see why you might not want your customers eating one of Bessie's chocolates if they were prepared in a kitchen that wasn't sanitary."

"The town dump is more sanitary. No way! No way am I going to sell her chocolates and open myself up to a lawsuit. For all I care, she can beg and plead and cut my arm to shreds with her ridiculously sharp fingernails!"

Okay, now he was being a little overdramatic.

But he did have a point.

Just the idea of eating one of Bessie's chocolates made Hayley's stomach turn. There was no way Hayley was ever going to try one.

Famous last words.

Chapter 5

When Hayley carried her two heavy bags of groceries out of the store, she immediately regretted not wheeling them out in a cart. She forgot she had parked her car at the far end of the parking lot that snaked around the side of the store. She decided to tough it out. At least holding the handles of her reuseable bags might develop her upper-body strength. It certainly wouldn't be because of her time at the gym; she hadn't been to the gym in months.

Hayley reached her Kia and popped open the trunk. She lifted the bags with all her might and dropped them inside. Then she slammed the trunk shut. She was about to open the driver's-side door, when she heard a noise. She turned to where the sound was coming from. It was a guttural wail, like an injured animal's. It was coming from behind the store's large green Dumpster.

Hayley took a step forward.

She spotted a bit of a bright flowery print.

Bessie's blouse.

Bessie was hiding behind the Dumpster.

More wailing.

More sobbing.

Then a sucking sound as Bessie tried to catch her breath.

Hayley frowned and marched over behind the Dumpster to find Bessie blowing her nose into a wad of used napkins, which Hayley prayed she hadn't picked out of the Dumpster.

Hayley put a comforting hand on Bessie's shoulder. Bessie jumped, startled, and took a round-house swing at Hayley. Hayley staggered back; Bessie's pudgy fist missed her nose by inches.

"Bessie, relax! It's only me, Hayley."

Bessie squinted through her tears. "Oh, Hayley. Sorry. I thought you might be a rapist trying to take advantage of my frail condition."

"Frail" was not a word Hayley would ever associate with Bessie.

"What are you doing behind this Dumpster?" Hayley asked.

"Ron upset me so much. Made me feel like a freak. He said nobody in his right mind would ever eat one of my chocolates. He just wouldn't listen to anything I had to say. Nobody ever does. I can see people's eyes glaze over whenever I strike up a conversation with them. Or the looks on people's faces when I approach, as if they're saying to themselves, 'Oh, God, here comes Bessie Winthrop. How am I going to get around having to talk to her?' It's awful, Hayley, just awful."

"Bessie, you know that's not true."

"You're just trying to make me feel better. I know it. Ron couldn't have been more dismissive. And when I left the store, I just lost it. I was so distraught—I wanted to throw up. That's been happening ever since middle school when that nasty Sabrina Merryweather teased me for having four Jell-O pudding pops in my *Saved by the Bell* lunch pail. Anyway, I was standing outside the automatic doors of the store and I just started to dry heave right in front of everyone trying to come in and shop. I was so embarrassed that I ran around to the side of the building and took refuge behind this Dumpster, where nobody can see me. And I'm just waiting it out until I can calm down and walk home with at least a shred of dignity."

"Where's your car?"

"At home in my driveway. It's kaput. Needs a new engine, which I can't afford. I was hoping if Ron sold my chocolates, maybe they'd become popular and I might make enough money to pay for the car repair."

"Bessie, let me drive you home."

Bessie stopped crying and looked at Hayley.

Grateful someone was finally taking at least a slight interest in her.

"That's so kind of you, Hayley. Thank you."

Hayley steadied Bessie with a gentle hand under her arm and guided her over to her car. Bessie plopped into the passenger seat and struggled with the seat belt. She began a verbal tirade about how the car companies conspired against plus-size women with ample bosoms by not making the straps longer. When she finished, her tears were gone and she was downright chatty as Hayley drove her to her tiny house on Ledgelawn Avenue.

As they pulled up in front of Bessie's house, Bessie reached out with her long fingernails and touched Hayley's coat. "Thank you so much for the ride home. Would you like to come in for a cup of coffee?"

Hayley had to admit she was curious to see the inside of the house and if Ron's wife was exaggerating about Bessie's living conditions.

But she wanted to get home.

"Sorry, Bessie, I've got three cuts of very expensive steaks I need to broil for dinner tonight. I'm celebrating. Got a temporary raise at work today."

Bessie's eyes lit up. "Congratulations! Then I insist you come in . . . just for a few minutes. I made some of my homemade chocolate truffles today. You can take them home as a dessert."

Bessie looked so happy to have someone to talk to, even if only for a few minutes. Hayley relented. She shut off the car and got out. Bessie was still struggling to free herself from the seat belt, so

Hayley went around to assist her and then they walked up to the house.

Bessie unlocked the front door and ushered her guest inside. Hayley stepped into the darkened foyer and was suddenly overwhelmed by a nauseating stench. She could barely breathe. Bessie flipped on the lights. Ron's soon-to-be ex-wife, Lenora, was definitely not exaggerating. The hallway was lined with boxes of books and junk and old clothing and knickknacks.

"Let me put the coffeepot on," Bessie said, having to turn sideways in order to squeeze through the small pathway to the kitchen. Hayley followed.

The kitchen was a disaster area. Dishes and pots and pans were piled high in the sink. Litter boxes, which hadn't been cleaned out, lined up around the walls and underneath the small kitchen table. The upholstery on the chairs was ripped and torn and the stuffing was hanging out.

And then there were the cats.

Dozens of them.

All shapes and sizes.

Pouring in from all different directions.

Jumping up on the counter.

Rubbing up against Hayley's leg.

The cacophony of meows was almost deafening. Hayley could not believe her eyes. Bessie was too busy scooping spoonfuls of coffee grounds into the top of her coffeemaker to notice the three cats bunched up together on the counter and licking her hand.

"I don't have many friends, Hayley," Bessie said, closing the top of the coffeemaker and pushing the start button. "I appreciate you being so nice to me."

"I'm your friend, Bessie," Hayley said, her heart breaking.

"Do you mean that?"

"Yes. Absolutely."

Bessie smiled and then pulled a key out of the pocket of her polyester tan slacks and pressed it into the palm of Hayley's hand.

"What's this?" Hayley asked.

"The key to my heart."

Hayley's face fell and Bessie cackled.

"I'm kidding. It's a key to my house."

Hayley gave her a puzzled look.

"I have nightmares, every once in a while, that something's going to happen to me, like I might kick the bucket while watching *Duck Dynasty* and nobody even notices I'm not around town for, like, weeks or months, and then finally the house starts to smell. . . ."

Starts *to smell?*

"And it gets so bad the fire department has to break the door down and they find me dead in my recliner, stiff and decomposing, and the cats have eaten my face off because they're so hungry. I've heard stories of that happening, you know."

Hayley nodded, horrified at the thought.

"So now that I have a friend looking out for me, I want her to have a key so she can check up on me. Just in case."

Hayley opened her mouth to protest. She didn't think she was ready to be Bessie's caretaker; but then she saw Bessie's face, hopeful and excited that she finally found someone who actually cared enough to keep tabs on her.

Or cared at all.

Hayley pocketed the key. "What are friends for?"

Bessie beamed from ear to ear.

Bessie picked up a small box. This one was wrapped in yellow cellophane. She blew the cat hair off the top of it before handing it to Hayley. "Here are the truffles I promised for you and the kids. Enjoy!"

Hayley stared at the box and forced a smile on her face. "Yummy."

Chapter 6

Hayley stared at the blank computer screen as she cradled her laptop while sitting up in her bed.

Her column was due in the morning and she still hadn't come up with a topic to write about, let alone a recipe to include at the end.

Chocolate, however, was on her mind a lot lately. Especially since she was including chocolate-based recipes in all her columns for the entire month of February in celebration of Valentine's Day.

But she was finding it hard to concentrate. Mostly because she was worried about Gemma. When Hayley got home from Bessie's house, Gemma was already barricaded in her room and didn't want to eat any supper. Hayley tried to get her to talk about what was wrong, but Gemma once again refused.

Hayley set her laptop down on the comforter

of her bed and leaned back against the pillows she had propped up against the headboard.

She sighed.

What was she going to write about?

She checked the digital clock on the DVR, which rested underneath her tiny television on the dresser. Almost midnight.

She thought about knocking lightly on Gemma's door to see if she was still awake and trying to talk to her again.

Perhaps the third time would be the charm.

But she wasn't going to hold her breath.

Hayley crawled out of bed and pulled up her knotted gray sweatpants, which were threatening to slide off her waist. At least they weren't too tight. Worrying about her daughter's sullen mood had caused her to drop a few pounds.

Every crisis had a silver lining.

She walked out into the second-floor hallway and noticed through the crack under Gemma's bedroom door that the lights in her room were off. She decided against waking her. Dustin's room was dark as well. It was very unusual for her kids to be asleep before midnight. They would always make a big production out of finishing their homework and going to sleep on a school night, but inevitably it was all just a show for their mother to keep her happy. Instead, they would hide under the bedcovers, playing a handheld video game or texting their friends.

Hayley turned to go back in her room, when she heard a strange sound coming from downstairs.

It was a hacking cough.

And wheezing.

Followed by faint whimpering.

Leroy.

Hayley bounded for the stairs. She thought it was odd that Leroy hadn't followed her up to her room earlier when she went to write her column. He never liked having her out of his sight when she was home.

When she hit the first-floor landing and turned the corner toward the kitchen, the lights were off and it was pitch-dark. She stepped on a bone she had picked up for Leroy and a sharp pain shot through the sole of her foot. She yelped and cursed to herself as she felt the side of the wall for a light switch in the kitchen.

There was a continuous violent heaving now. When her fingers finally found the switch and she bathed the kitchen in bright light, Hayley gasped.

Leroy was crouched down, throwing up all over the kitchen floor. Her eyes went straight to the ripped and crumpled yellow cellophane that Bessie had used to wrap her homemade truffles. It was lying next to her little dog's spasming body.

The box had been torn open and what few chocolates were left were scattered about the floor.

Oh, my God.

Leroy had eaten almost all of them.

And everyone knows chocolate can be severely toxic to a dog.

Hayley raced to the poor little guy and instinctively tried to pick him up, but he backed away. His tiny body was shaking, and then he threw up some more brown muddy chunks and liquid.

She couldn't understand it. She had carefully placed the box on the kitchen counter, well out of Leroy's reach.

That's when she noticed Blueberry.

He was sitting calmly on the counter; his tail was curled underneath his massive body.

A relaxed, almost serene look was on his face.

She instantly knew what had happened.

Blueberry tore the cellophane off the box with his claws and knocked it to the floor, where a curious Leroy was waiting to explore what was inside. And given the opportunity, Leroy would eat just about anything he could get his paws on.

What disturbed Hayley most was the barely perceptible smile on Blueberry's face. It was like he was enjoying the commotion he caused.

By now, both of Hayley's kids had heard all the noise downstairs and were in the kitchen with their mother assessing the situation.

They all instantly came to the same conclusion.

"Blueberry is trying to murder Leroy!" Dustin yelled.

Gemma dropped to her knees and began frantically petting Leroy's back. Her eyes were brimming with tears. "Is he going to die, Mom?"

Hayley shook her head. "No!"

She was praying she was going to be right.

There was a lull in Leroy's wheezing and heaving, so Hayley scooped him up in her arms and raced for the door leading out to her driveway.

"Gemma, come with me. I need you to drive for me while I hold Leroy. Dustin, call Dr. Winston and tell him we're on our way over to his office and it's an emergency. After that, stay here and look after Blueberry."

"I'm not getting near that thing. He's like the feline version of Jeffrey Dahmer!"

"Just do it!" she barked as she was halfway out the door, with Gemma on her heels, the car keys jangling in her hand.

Hayley knew time was of the essence.

And she kept telling herself Leroy would make it through this.

They all would.

Chapter 7

Hayley and Gemma burst through the door of Dr. Winston's veterinary clinic. Leroy was shaking as Hayley clutched him against her bosom, rubbing his fur to keep him warm. She was shivering herself, since she had left the house in a panic and forgot to bring her coat. Hayley was now in a wrinkled green t-shirt and sweatpants. Gemma raced ahead of her and began pounding her fist on the reception desk.

"Help! We need help out here!"

Within seconds a pretty young girl, not that many years older than Gemma, ran out from the back. She was wearing pink scrubs and white bunny slippers. She introduced herself as the doctor's assistant.

Mary.

Or Marnie.

Hayley wasn't really listening. She was too worried about Leroy.

The assistant gently took Leroy from Hayley, requested that they take a seat in the waiting room, and then whisked the ailing Shih Tzu into the back, leaving a distraught Hayley and a teary-eyed Gemma.

They plopped down next to each other on a hard couch and just stared into space. They didn't talk for what seemed like hours.

Hayley kept telling herself that Dr. Winston was the best animal doctor in New England. He had been the town's vet since Hayley was in middle school. She couldn't even begin to count the number of pets she had raised over the years whom he had treated.

Dr. Winston would know what to do.

Leroy would be back to his old self in no time.

She could not even fathom any alternative scenario. Leroy was her best hope of surviving empty-nest syndrome after the kids left for college. She knew that when that day came, she would be completely alone for the first time in her entire life. Hayley always imagined Leroy would be her closest companion at home, and would get her through the inevitable loneliness that was sure to crop up from time to time.

But he ate almost an entire box of chocolates.

That much chocolate could kill a dog.

She read it somewhere.

Hayley tried to shake the unpleasant thoughts out of her head.

She was not going to allow her mind to go there.

Finally the assistant came shuffling out again.

Hayley couldn't take her eyes off the girl's adorable furry bunny slippers. The eyes were tiny bells that made a jangling sound as she walked.

Too cute.

"Mary, how's Leroy?" Hayley asked, jumping to her feet.

Gemma quickly followed suit.

"I don't know. The doctor didn't tell me. But he's ready to see you now," she said.

Hayley's heart skipped a beat. She was desperate for some kind of reassurance and this girl wasn't giving her any.

"And my name's Marla," she added, holding the door open for Hayley. "Marla Heasley."

"I'm sorry. I'm usually good with names. I'm just a little upset and distracted right now. I'm sure you understand."

Marla didn't say a word.

Apparently, she didn't understand.

But Hayley was in no condition to worry about the feelings of Dr. Winston's new assistant. She blew past her toward the doctor's office. Gemma grabbed some facial tissues off the receptionist's desk and blew her nose loudly as she followed her mother.

The door to Dr. Winston's office was open, so Hayley barged right in to learn Leroy's prognosis.

She stopped dead in her tracks so fast, Gemma bumped into her from behind.

Dr. Winston wasn't sitting behind his desk.

He wasn't there at all.

Instead, she found a disheveled man in his midthirties, with mussed hair and thick glasses. He was wearing a stained white lab coat over plaid men's pajamas. His bare feet were up on the desk as he perused a file. A pair of gray flip-flops were lying on the floor next to the desk, where he had dropped them.

"Who are you?" Hayley found herself saying.

He quickly put his feet down and cleared his throat, trying to act as professional as possible. "Sorry. I'm Dr. Palmer."

He reached a hand across the desk to shake hers.

Hayley took it limply, uninterested in pleasantries. "How's Leroy?"

"One sick dog, I'm afraid. But he'll be fine."

Hayley exhaled a deep breath; a wave of relief spread through her entire body as she fell down into a chair across from Dr. Palmer. Gemma finally stopped crying and sat quietly down in a chair next to her mother.

"As you know, chocolate contains theobromine, a stimulant that can sometimes affect the central nervous system of a canine. Leroy ate enough to poison a much larger dog, so the situation was quite serious. Fortunately, I treated him with activated charcoal, which slows down the absorption, and now I am administering an intravenous fluid therapy to flush out the remaining toxins. He's responding, but I'd like to keep him overnight under observation."

"So he's going to make it?" Hayley said, gripping the edge of the desk.

Dr. Palmer nodded. "No reason he won't make a full recovery. Brave little guy. Never complained once."

Gemma smiled for the first time in a month and grabbed her mother's hand. "Oh, thank God!"

Hayley smiled back at her.

Finally a nice mother-daughter moment.

But then Gemma quickly realized she was supposed to be depressed and snatched her hand away from her mother and went back to moping.

The awkward moment was not lost on Dr. Palmer. However, he chose to ignore it. "Just promise me you'll keep anything containing chocolate out of Leroy's reach from here on in."

Hayley wanted to explain that she was not an irresponsible pet owner. It was a homicidal, heartless cat she had recently taken in who was responsible for Leroy's near-death experience. It seemed too silly to bring that up, so she kept it to herself.

She decided to change the subject. "Are you filling in for Dr. Winston while he's on vacation?"

"Oh, you didn't hear?" Dr. Palmer asked, setting Leroy's file down on the desk. "Dr. Winston retired. Moved to Florida with his wife to be closer to the grandkids. I took over his practice just this past week."

"So you're here permanently?"

"Guess you're stuck with me," he said, grinning.

He had a nice smile.

And soulful green eyes.

Hayley caught herself staring at him.

"Sorry for my appearance. I was already sleeping when your son called my emergency hotline. Or as I like to call it, the Batphone. It sounded quite serious, so I didn't bother getting dressed. I just texted my assistant to meet me here and raced on over. I bought a house just a few doors down from the clinic."

Hayley nodded. He had such a nice complexion. Maybe he was older, in his forties even, and just looked like he was in his thirties. Though she couldn't tell from the baggy pajamas he was wearing, she was betting there was a nice physique underneath.

Gemma started to stand up. "Well, thank you for everything, Dr. Palmer."

"Are you from around here?" Hayley asked, not making a move to get up.

"Grew up in Portland. But then I moved to California to go to Stanford."

Stanford.

Smart too.

"Then UC Davis School of Veterinary Medicine before starting a practice in LA. But honestly, after ten years, I missed the seasons, the fall foliage, everything I loved about growing up in New England. So I had been looking for an excuse to come back, and that's when I heard about Dr. Winston's plan to retire."

"Well, you're going to love living in Bar Harbor," Hayley said, giggling.

Giggle? Really? Did I actually just giggle?

"I used to come here a lot as a kid. Not a lot of places have this kind of charm. It's a really special place. I'm just happy to be back in Maine. I hear you spend half your life trying to get out of the state and the second half of your life trying to get back."

He winked at Hayley.

At least she hoped he was winking and didn't have something in his eye.

Damn, this guy is attractive.

Gemma moved to the door of the office. "We'll come by tomorrow to pick up Leroy."

Hayley still didn't make a move to leave. "If you have any questions about the town, don't hesitate to call me. I work at the *Island Times*."

"Oh, I know who you are. First thing I did when I arrived in town was to buy the paper and I became an instant fan of your column."

"You like to cook?"

"I can't boil water. But it sure is refreshing reading someone who is as passionate about food as I am."

Oh, this one is good.

What a smooth talker.

Hayley found herself giggling again. Like a schoolgirl.

She threw a hand over her mouth to stop herself.

What an utterly humiliating moment.

But Dr. Palmer didn't seem to mind at all.

Gemma, however, did mind. In a big way.

"Mom, can we go now?" she whined.

Hayley finally stood up and thanked Dr. Palmer again. "I mean it. If you have any questions—"

"I know where to find you," he said, winking again.

No. He definitely didn't have anything stuck in his eye. He was absolutely, without question, winking at her and it was making her heart flutter.

She was on cloud nine as she walked outside to the car.

Luckily, Gemma was with her to slap her back to reality.

"Well, that was totally embarrassing," Gemma said.

"Gemma, just because you're in a foul mood, you don't have to take it out on me, okay?"

"Fine. But before you get all worked up about this guy, there's something you should know. . . ."

"I'm not worked up. I don't get worked up."

"He's married."

"What?"

"While you were staring at him with those

googly eyes, I was looking at the framed photo on his desk of himself with his wife and kids."

"Oh. Seriously?"

"Yes, Mom."

"Well, thanks for noticing. You saved me from making a fool of myself."

"Don't mention it."

Gemma tossed the car keys to her mother, got in the passenger side, and slammed the door shut.

Hayley took one last look at the vet clinic.

She could see Dr. Palmer through the window into the reception area of the clinic. He looked adorable in his plaid pajamas and was scribbling something on a notepad.

That was a close one. A married guy?

Forget it. Best just to stick to her current plan of not dating, or, better yet, not even getting within close proximity of any man she found remotely interesting.

It was too bad that place where Wonder Woman grew up, Paradise Island, where no men were allowed among the Amazons, wasn't taking reservations.

Island Food & Spirits
by
Hayley Powell

Recently our beloved family dog, Leroy, scared us all when he devoured something he wasn't supposed to eat, and we had to rush him to the vet. We were all worried sick, since he is such an important part of our family. But I am pleased to report the little bugger is doing just fine. When I finally got home from that horrifying ordeal and settled in for the night, my mind wandered back to another time some years back when I suffered another big scare.

Dustin was around seven years old and in second grade. As usual we were running late for school and work. On the drive to Emer-

son Conners Middle School, I
suddenly remembered that I
forgot to pack Dustin a lunch.
So I told him to get into my
purse, which was on the seat
beside him in the backseat of the
car, and take out a five-dollar bill
so he could buy himself a hot
lunch in the cafeteria. He was
thrilled because with five bucks
he could afford to purchase his
favorite chicken fingers. Salads
have never been too popular in
our family.

Later, around lunchtime, my
cell phone rang while I was at the
office. It was the school nurse
and she was frantic. She told
me she had six very nauseous
little boys in her office, including
my own son, Dustin, and that I
needed to come pick him up as
soon as possible.

I dashed out of my office and
raced to the school, praying
there wasn't another flu bug
going around, because I just
couldn't afford to take any personal days to care for him at
home. I had to get him out of

that virus-infested school as fast as I could.

After parking the car and racing to the nurse's office, I burst through the door and came to a screeching halt in the reception area as five other mothers were standing there, all staring daggers at me. I looked at the crying boys and the angry parents and thought, *How could a flu bug be my fault?* Dustin was perfectly healthy when I dropped him off at school earlier!

The school nurse informed me that she had determined through questioning that Dustin had brought candy to school and had passed it out to his friends. I said that was not possible because there was absolutely no candy in our house! I knew that for a fact because it was just the night before that I had finished off the last of the Mini Snickers Bars, which I kept hidden in my bedroom closet. So there was no possible way Dustin could have gotten his hands on them. But all the boys admitted to eating candy and that it was Dustin who gave it to them.

I knelt down on the floor in front of a sniffling Dustin, who rocked back and forth, looking scared to death and a little pale. I gently asked him where he got the candy everyone was talking about. After a few minutes of me reassuring him I wouldn't get mad, he finally told me he found some mints in my purse while he was getting his lunch money. I was totally baffled. I turned to the parents and told them I most certainly did not have any mints, gum, or candy in my purse and I had no idea what my son was talking about. Six little boys, all sniffling and holding their tummies, kept nodding and insisting that "yes, yes," I did.

I asked Dustin if he had any of these so-called mints left. He nodded and reached in his back pocket and pulled out a small box. I heard the gasp from the other mothers behind me before I saw the package that Dustin was holding in his chubby little hands. The mothers started shouting. The boys cried louder. The nurse called the principal's office.

I grabbed the package out of Dustin's hand and simply stared at it in horror as I felt the blood rush to my face. I knew exactly what it was. It was my box of birth control pills, which I had just opened the night before. I will refrain from telling you why.

I tried to make light of this ghastly situation. "Well, at least we won't have to worry about our boys getting pregnant." No one seemed to appreciate the joke.

There was nothing else left to do but stand up, grab Dustin's hand, and make a mad dash out the door past all of the upset parents, offering my apologies over my shoulder as we fled to the doctor's office.

All I could think about on the drive to the hospital emergency room was what harm could this possibly do to my beloved little boy? Oh, Lord, I hoped it wouldn't affect him in any way physically.

I already had one girl at home on the crest of adolescence, who I knew in my bones was going to be one moody teenager when she grew up.

Luckily everything turned out for the best. Some upset stomachs, but no permanent damage. No one had any allergies, so that was a relief.

Dustin and I had a very in-depth discussion about not taking any more items out of my purse other than the ones he has permission to remove. I felt we dodged a bullet.

I just hoped that the other mothers would eventually feel the same way, but I wasn't holding out much hope. I dreaded the next PTA meeting.

Well, for me, the best way to end a day of crisis is with a really great cocktail (or two). And I'm also going to prepare a delicious chocolate appetizer to share at Liddy's niece's baby shower tomorrow evening. I'm just thankful it's not my son having the baby shower!

Hot-Pepper Martini

<u>Ingredients</u>
3 ounces pepper-infused vodka
8 drops grenadine
Juice of 1 lime
6 fresh pitted cherries

Combine your vodka, grenadine, and lime juice in a cocktail shaker filled with ice. Strain into two chilled martini glasses, then garnish with cherries. Sit back, relax, and enjoy!

Chocolate Chip Cheese Ball

<u>Ingredients</u>
1 package (8 ounces) cream cheese, softened
½ cup butter, softened (not margarine)
¾ cup confectioners' sugar
2 to 3 tablespoons brown sugar
1 teaspoon vanilla extract
1 cup miniature chocolate chips
¾ cup pecans (or your favorite nuts), chopped

In a mixing bowl, beat cream cheese and butter until creamy. Add sugars and vanilla and mix until well combined. Stir in your chocolate chips. Cover and refrigerate for at least two hours. Gather together the cold mixture into a ball and cover with plastic wrap. Chill for at least another hour. Roll the ball in the chopped pecans just before serving. Serve with butter or shortbread cookies or any flavor graham cracker.

Chapter 8

Bank teller Pam Innsbrook's normally warm and sweet face was particularly strained this morning as she tried to ignore the shouting coming from an office on the other side of the large open lobby of the First National Bank. The teller was processing Hayley's paycheck from the *Island Times* as a deposit into Hayley's account.

"Going to be a cold one out there today," Pam said with a forced smile as she handed Hayley her receipt.

"At least it's not snowing," Hayley said, her words drowned out by the yelling.

"I'm sorry, what did you say, Hayley? I didn't hear you."

"I said at least it's not snowing!" she shouted.

"Oh yes, right," Pam said, her smile slowly sinking into a frown as she glanced across the lobby at the two people engaged in an epic battle of four-letter words and finger pointing inside a glass-walled office.

Hayley glanced behind her and saw Bessie Winthrop, her massive frame nearly pinning the bank's wiry loan officer, Cody Donovan, up against the wall in his office. Her pudgy index finger was so close to his face that it was threatening to poke out his eye.

Cody squinted and squirmed, desperate to be free of this unbelievable force of nature, but Bessie wasn't going anywhere.

All eyes in the bank were drawn to Bessie's splashy-colored Hawaiian print muumuu, which spruced up the dullish beige walls of Cody's office.

Cody tried to make a break for it, but Bessie anticipated the move, and used her considerable bulk to keep him trapped against the wall. Cody's sudden move had caused Bessie's finger to lodge up one of his nostrils, and a few chuckles erupted in the bank as it appeared Bessie was picking Cody's nose.

Cody whipped his face sharply to the left and Bessie managed to yank her finger out of his nose and then wiped her whole hand on her muumuu as she screamed, "I'm tired of you talking down to me, you sniveling corporate scumbag! I demand you take me seriously!"

"If you don't get out of my office right now, I'll have you physically removed!"

Easier said than done.

Hayley glanced outside to see Sid, the security guard, crossing the street. In his hand there was a paper cup of piping-hot coffee purchased from the diner directly adjacent to the bank. She didn't want him overreacting and having Bessie arrested, so Hayley decided to take matters into her own hands.

She stuffed the deposit receipt into her coat pocket, thanked Pam, and then scooted across the lobby and into Cody Donovan's office.

"Morning, Cody. Morning, Bessie."

They both looked at her, dumbfounded for a moment.

The fear and tension slowly drained from Cody's face.

Help at last.

"I don't mean to interrupt, Bessie, but I just had to tell you how much I enjoyed the truffles you gave me yesterday. They were so yummy! I may just have to buy some more from you."

Hayley thought it best not to mention her dog nearly dying because of her blasted candies. Hayley's sole mission now was to lower the heat on this very hot situation.

Bessie grinned from ear to ear.

"Oh, I'm so pleased you liked them, Hayley," Bessie cooed, before looking back at Cody and scowling. "See, I'm not a fruitcake. I have real talent."

Cody ignored her. His eyes were fixed on Hayley. "You look younger every time I see you, Hayley. So pretty . . ."

His voice trailed off as he stared at her. He had this rather wolfish smile on his face, which made Hayley extremely uncomfortable.

She and Cody had dated briefly in high school during junior year. Nothing serious. He was a basketball player, even though he was on the short side. She was a cheerleader for one season before they started doing more elaborate routines involving pyramids and cartwheels. Then Hayley dropped out and joined something less physically intense, like glee club. But then they started doing these complicated dance routines, so Hayley just decided to focus less on extracurricular activities.

Cody finally tore his eyes off Hayley and glared at Bessie. "Look, I've told you a hundred times. It's never going to happen, so you might as well get used to it."

Bessie's face scrunched up and her face turned a bright shade of red. "You know what I could get used to? Seeing your head go through that glass window. Then when you're on the floor, lying on your back, with your face cut to pieces, I could take a shard of the broken glass and stab you in the heart with it about a thousand times. Yeah, I could get used to that!"

Cody reached for the phone on his desk. "I'm calling the police."

Hayley put a hand out to stop him. "No, Cody. Please. Don't. Bessie's just upset. She'll leave quietly. Right, Bessie?"

Hayley turned to Bessie, who was contemplating her next move. It looked like she just might go through with her initial plan of smashing Cody's head through the glass wall.

But finally she backed down.

"I'm only leaving because Hayley is my friend and she's just here to help. I'm sorry you got mixed up in all my personal drama, Hayley. You're a good friend," Bessie said, straightening her muumuu, wiping the sweat off her face with her manicured purple-painted nails, and then waddling out of the office.

"Call me later, girlfriend," Bessie said, her head held high as she marched toward the double doors, ignoring all the stares from the bank employees and customers.

Hayley suddenly noticed she was still touching Cody's hand and tried to pull it away, but he was too fast for her and grabbed it. He caressed it gently with his other hand. "I always remember your soft hands."

Hayley tried wriggling her hand free from his grasp, but he held it more tightly.

"Thank you, Hayley. That woman needs to learn some manners."

"What were you two fighting about?"

"It's not worth getting into. Suffice it to say, she's a public nuisance and nobody in town should take her seriously."

"Bessie is my friend," Hayley said, trying once more to yank her hand free from his grip and once again failing. "And I'd really like to know why she was so upset."

"I don't want to talk about her anymore. I want to talk about you. I heard Lex Bansfield left town to take a job in Vermont. So, am I to understand that you are now on the market again?" Cody asked. His wolfish smile was getting bigger.

Suddenly a woman's voice drifted in from the doorway to the office. "I hope I'm not too early for our lunch, Cody."

Cody's hands grew cold as he turned to face his wife, Kerry, a formidable, strong woman, bigger than Hayley, whose imposing nature just about rivaled Bessie's. She had a dark complexion, with long, jet-black hair pulled into a bun. She was wearing a bright yellow business suit, even though she didn't have a job. She just liked to look professional as a banker's wife.

Kerry's eyes were locked on her husband and Hayley holding hands.

Cody let go of Hayley as though he had been touching a red-hot stove-top burner.

"I see you two are catching up on old times. How special," Kerry said in a low, steady, ominous voice.

Kerry also went to high school with Cody and Hayley and had her sights set on Cody when he had shared an apple with her in the lunchroom. But it took Cody a while longer to get up to speed with Kerry's plans to marry him. So Kerry was acutely aware of all the women he had pursued before finally settling down with her.

Especially the flirty cheerleader he was head over heels for during junior year.

Hayley.

Even after their wedding, Kerry never went out of her way to be friendly with Hayley. She always saw her as that long-lost first love of her husband's— the one still lurking about town, divorced, with no man in her life. A woman who at any moment in time could decide to prey upon Kerry's husband once again.

Kerry Donovan was going to remain vigilant and keep a watchful eye on this potential threat to her security.

The past was going to stay just that.

The past, if she had anything to say about it.

Hayley wanted to reassure Cody's wife that she was only sixteen when this overblown relationship occurred with Kerry's future husband. The whole affair had barely lasted a month. In fact, it basically amounted to three dates and a fumbled grope in the backseat of a 1983 Oldsmobile.

But it probably wasn't wise to try and reason with Kerry Donovan at that moment.

Especially since Hayley had just been caught holding Cody's hand.

Chapter 9

Hayley was grateful for the distraction when Bessie barged through the door to the *Island Times*. She was bundled up in her bright pink parka, which made her look like a giant bottle of Pepto-Bismol with tiny legs.

Sal and the few full-time reporters on staff had already gone home for the weekend, leaving Hayley alone to work on Bruce's column in his absence.

She still hadn't figured out what to write about. There were zero crimes to report. The police scanner she kept on top of the refrigerator at home was so quiet she thought she had left it unplugged.

No missing bicycles.

No broken windows.

All in all, a typical boring mid-February week in Bar Harbor.

Bessie threw her arms open to hug Hayley, forcing Hayley to stand up from her desk. Bessie grabbed her so hard that Hayley audibly gasped, and her face was buried so deep in Bessie's pink coat she could barely breathe.

"I just stopped by to thank you, Hayley," Bessie said, still squeezing her.

"For what?" Hayley managed to squeak out with her last bit of breath.

"If you hadn't shown up at the bank, I would've decked that weasel, Cody Donovan. And now I'd be in a local jail cell eating a cold ham sandwich, with wilted lettuce and mayo past the expiration date, cooling my jets and worried about my cats."

Bessie certainly had the talent to paint a mental picture.

"What were you two fighting about?" Hayley asked.

"His itty-bitty, tiny penis," Bessie said with a guffaw. She was honking with laughter.

For a split second, Hayley thought she was serious.

By some stretch of the imagination, were Bessie and Cody sexually involved? It seemed so random, so unexpected. But in a small town full of juicy secrets, it was entirely possible.

"No, I'm kiddin' ya, Hayley. I wouldn't be caught dead rubbing bellies with that grade-A loser. Not me. I have some taste when it comes to men."

Running in her mind through the list of local men she knew Bessie had dated over the years, Hayley thought it best not to comment on Bessie's wildly deluded opinion of the gentlemen from her past.

"But his little penis is my official reason for our argument and I'm spreading it all over town," Bessie said with a big smile on her face. "Because I won't rest until I humiliate that lying, power-hungry prick!"

"Do you really think that's a good idea, Bessie?"

"Probably not, but I'm at my wit's end, and it's better to attack first than be attacked. Plus you know he's going to blab all over town that I'm this unstable, uncouth loudmouth, and we both know that's definitely *not* true!"

Again, best not to comment right at this moment.

Hayley wanted to press Bessie further to find out what she and Cody were fighting about at the bank, but she had the distinct feeling Bessie, like Cody, had no interest in talking about the real reason they had nearly come to blows.

Suddenly Bessie stuck her small pudgy hand in Hayley's face and latched onto her chin, pulling her closer. Bessie puckered up and planted a big kiss on Hayley's cheek, leaving a bright red lipstick smear.

"Don't worry. I'm not looking for any lesbian action. I totally like boys. Except for one time in my twenties after one too many Fireball whiskey shots with my Weight Watchers sponsor, who had the hots for me."

"Okay," Hayley said, not sure where this was going.

"I'm just in a really good mood, and I love you for being my friend, Hayley, and I had this huge brainstorm after I saw you at the bank and I rushed right over here to tell you."

"What is it?"

"Hayley's Kisses," Bessie said, grinning from ear to ear, her eyes wide with excitement.

"I don't get it."

"A new recipe I came up with for a line of chocolates that I plan to sell, once I get my new business up and running."

Hayley suddenly had a notion of what Bessie and Cody were probably fighting about. Bessie desperately wanted to start a candy-making business, and Cody was one of two bank loan officers in town.

"And I want to name this soon-to-be best-selling candy after my closest friend," Bessie cooed.

"Bessie, I'm flattered. That's very sweet of you," Hayley said.

And she meant it.

She was genuinely touched by the gesture.

"I wanted you to be the first to know. I feel it

in my bones, Hayley. This one's going to finally put me on the map."

"Fingers crossed," Hayley said hopefully.

"I better get home and feed my cats. I'll call you once I whip up my first batch because, of course, I want you to be the first person in the world to try one."

She hugged Hayley again—this time more gently and less bone crushing—and hurried out the door. Hayley watched her scuttle down the sidewalk to her car, fumbling in the pockets of her bright pink parka for her keys. Just as she fished them out and unlocked her car with the remote, she was intercepted by a man twice her size. At least in height.

Hayley recognized him immediately.

Wolf Conway.

One of Bessie's ex-boyfriends.

Wolf was a lumbering Paul Bunyan type of guy. Roughly six-four, he had a bushy red beard and freckles all over his face. He wore a brown wool cap, a black-and-red-plaid coat, paint-splattered jeans, and tan work boots. Hayley was surprised Wolf hadn't yet given her a topic to write about in Bruce's crime column, given the big man's long record of public intoxication and disturbing the peace.

Yes, Bessie's taste in men was exemplary.

He spoke to her animatedly, waving his arms in

front of her face so much that she had to duck a few times to avoid getting slapped.

Wolf had a violent temper; that was the chief reason Bessie broke it off with him a few years back. In fact, she stopped all contact. And the scuttlebutt was she even took out a restraining order against him. Clearly, if that was the case, Wolf wasn't adhering to the rules at this moment.

Wolf could barely hold down a job. Hayley remembered he worked at the docks, towing the lines of some of the fishermen's boats for a while. Recently he was a fry cook at a local burger joint and made a mean plate of onion rings. Hayley had tried them once—they were greasy and good. But he got sacked about a month ago for mouthing off to the customers one too many times. Now he was living off his unemployment check, trying to make ends meet. Hayley heard Wolf had lost his little shack on the outskirts of town through foreclosure.

Wolf was yelling now and Bessie tried to push past him to her car, but he grabbed a fistful of her pink coat in his giant paw. She tried freeing herself from his grip and lost her balance and stumbled to the ground.

Hayley jumped up out of her chair and bolted out the door, not quite sure what she was going to do.

"Step away from her right now, Wolf!" Hayley said, her voice cracking from fear.

Wolf glared at Hayley for a moment, then down at Bessie, who was on her back, her fat arms and legs flailing in the air like an upended cockroach. Painted pink.

Bessie rolled on her side and reached out to try and kick Wolf in the shins with her black rubber snow boots. He just took a step back from her to avoid getting hit.

"I'm going to call the police right now," Hayley said, turning to head back inside.

Wolf took her threat seriously and stalked off.

Hayley rushed to Bessie's side and helped her to her feet, which was no easy task, given her heft. Bessie nearly went down again as Hayley hauled her upright from the sidewalk, nearly tearing her pink parka.

"Bessie, are you okay?"

"Only thing bruised is my ego. I can't believe I fell down like that. Especially in front of *him*. Oh, he makes my blood boil. Wish I had nailed him in the kneecaps."

Bessie's harsh words didn't hide the fact she was obviously shaken by her run-in with her ex.

"What did he want?" Hayley asked, steadying her and then bending down to pick up the car keys Bessie dropped during the scuffle.

"Wolf's just being Wolf, that's all. Nothing to

worry about. He still harbors a lot of resentment from the breakup. I broke the poor sucker's heart."

Hayley didn't quite believe what Bessie was saying. There seemed to be more to it than that. It had been a few years. She watched Bessie traipse off to her car and wondered what the real story was between Bessie and Wolf.

Chapter 10

"Dear God in heaven, they're leaving the island!" Hayley screamed as she sat wedged between Mona and Liddy in the front seat of Mona's pickup truck. They were tailgating a red Honda Accord as it cruised over the Trenton Bridge, which connected Mount Desert Island to the mainland.

"Faster, Mona, we're going to lose them," Liddy squealed.

"If I go any faster, I'll rear-end them," Mona barked. Her hands were gripping the steering wheel as they closed in on the Accord.

"I almost don't even want to know where they're going," Hayley wailed.

Hayley's worst fears were becoming a reality. She was coming to suspect that Gemma's withdrawal and her moodiness were far more serious than a failing grade or boy trouble. At this moment her only daughter was in the backseat of a car with a gang of local thugs and druggies. She was probably on her way to a meth lab operated out of a trailer in the woods outside of Bangor.

Or worse.

Hayley had heard all the stories: How one day your kid starts acting differently. No longer the bright, happy child who draws you a homemade Mother's Day card. Suddenly she's become a self-absorbed, rebellious, vicious troublemaker who no longer listens to anything you say. Now she misses her curfew, pals around with a seedy gang, smokes pot or heroin, forever lost to the dark side.

Okay, maybe she was being a little dramatic, but it was impossible not to allow her mind to go there.

Hayley yearned for the days when Gemma excitedly filled her in on even the tiniest details of her life. Now it was a Herculean task just getting her to offer more than a sullen look and a dismissive shrug.

Just twenty minutes earlier, Gemma grabbed her coat and was halfway out the back door before Hayley managed to stop her.

"Don't you think it's appropriate for me to know where you are going, Gemma?"

"I'm seventeen, Mom!" Gemma groaned.

"Exactly my point. You're still a year away from being of legal age, and until then I expect to know what you are doing, who you are with, and what time I can expect you home."

Gemma stomped her foot and sighed. "Fine! It's Tina Staples's birthday. Her parents are throwing her a surprise party, and I'm going with some friends. I'll be home by eleven. Happy now?"

Hayley breathed a sigh of relief. Tina was the daughter of Reverend Staples, the most trusted man in town. With the good reverend and his demure, soft-spoken wife, Edie, chaperoning, there would be no shenanigans going on. Hayley wouldn't need to worry about anything untoward occurring.

Hayley opened her mouth once again to try and find out what was bugging Gemma so much. Just then, though, a pair of headlights turned into the driveway.

"My ride's here," Gemma said, bolting out the door.

"Wait, you didn't tell me which friends!"

Hayley peered out the door to see Gemma jumping into the back of a Honda Accord. She didn't recognize any of the kids in the car when the interior lights snapped on. Especially troubling was the strapping boy behind the wheel. He was big and imposing, with a sly grin; his neck was craned around so he could look Gemma up and down with lustful eyes.

Well, Hayley couldn't see his eyes, but she knew in her bones they were probably full of lust.

Hayley wanted the names of everyone in that car; but by the time she made it out the door to the driveway, the Accord had already backed out and was roaring off down the street.

At that moment Mona's beat-up white truck pulled up to Hayley's house. Mona honked the horn. Hayley had completely forgotten she had plans to go to Randy's bar with Mona and Liddy for a cocktail.

Liddy rolled down the window and stuck her face out. "Next time we're taking my Mercedes. I just scratched my butt on a spring sticking out of Mona's upholstery."

"Stop your yammering and slide over for Hayley," Mona barked.

"Mona, the car you just passed, did you see who was driving?"

"No, it was too dark. Why?"

"I'm probably overreacting. I've just been a little concerned about Gemma lately and the kids she's been hanging around with. I hope she's not falling in with a bad crowd."

"Gemma's got a good head on her shoulders. She'll be fine," Mona said.

Mona was always so calm and reassuring.

"You're right. I mean, how much trouble can she possibly get into at Reverend Staples's house?" Hayley said.

"Is that where she told you she was going?" Liddy asked.

"Yes."

"Well, we just drove by the Staples' house. They're not home. All the lights were off," Liddy said.

"Oh, my God! She lied!" Hayley wailed.

Worst fears realized.

"Mona, follow that Accord!" Hayley said, opening the passenger-side door and trying to climb in, but Liddy pushed her back.

"No way am I sitting in the middle," Liddy said. "I'm claustrophobic! Besides, Mona smells like chicken grease."

"I just made dinner for my kids! Give me a friggin' break!" Mona spit out.

They lost a few precious seconds while Liddy got out and let Hayley squeeze in between them. Then Mona hit the accelerator and the white pickup zoomed down the street in hot pursuit of the Honda.

By the time they reached Ellsworth, ten minutes past the Trenton Bridge, Hayley was in full panic mode.

The Honda's right blinker clicked on and off as it pulled into a large parking lot. Mona veered her truck in behind them and then shut off her headlights so they wouldn't detect her tailing them.

"You think they're doing some kind of drug deal?" Liddy asked, unable to hide her excitement to be smack in the middle of such high-stakes drama.

"I know this place," Mona said. "I bring my older kids here all the time. It's the Beer 'n Bowl. Friday is psychedelic bowling night."

Hayley had heard of the Beer 'n Bowl. Bowling for the whole family. A bar area for the adults.

"Maybe they're going to rob the place!" Liddy said, smacking Hayley on the arm, proud of her new theory.

"Okay, you need to take a chill pill, Liddy, and stop scaring Hayley. I'm sure there's a reasonable explanation why she didn't just tell you she was coming here," Mona said.

"Why would she lie to me?" Hayley said, shaking her head.

They watched as five teenagers, Gemma included, piled out of the Accord. The big lug, who was behind the wheel, pulled something out of his coat pocket and started dispensing what looked like white pills to all the kids. They popped them into their mouths as they entered the bowling alley.

"They're getting high!" Hayley moaned, covering her face with her hands.

Liddy opened the door and jumped out, dragging Hayley by the sleeve behind her. "Come on, we have to get her out of there before she gets caught and arrested in a drug raid!"

As the three women entered, they were overwhelmed by neon spandex, bowling, glitter, and beer. It was like a disco circa 1978. Hayley looked around, but she didn't immediately spot Gemma and her gang of juvenile delinquents.

She turned to Liddy and Mona.

"Okay, I don't want her seeing us before we know exactly what's going on," Hayley said. "Why don't you two hang at the bar and act inconspicuous while I look around?"

"I *love* that idea," Liddy said with a big smile, turning to the bar and resting her eyes on the hot, young bartender shirtless underneath a tight leather vest. "More than you will ever know."

The bartender winked at Liddy. "Cougars in the house. Nice."

Liddy blushed and demurely touched his hand. "I'm way too young to be a cougar. Is there something else in the animal kingdom to describe a slightly older woman?"

"I *love* older women," the bartender said, caressing her hand.

"Okay, then. I guess technically I'm old enough to be a cougar," Liddy gushed.

"Just get us a couple of beers, okay, junior?" Mona barked, startling him.

He quickly grabbed a couple of glass mugs and began filling them from the tap.

Hayley had trouble scanning the crowd of bowlers with all the neon lighting and the reflections from the disco ball hanging over the lanes from the ceiling. She was halfway across the room when she suddenly spotted Gemma and her pals gathering in an area off to the side near the farthest bowling lane. Hayley was completely exposed just as Gemma unexpectedly turned in her direction.

Hayley ducked behind a family of five, all wearing matching red bowling shirts. She stayed low to the floor, looking through the father's legs at Gemma. Luckily, her daughter didn't see her. One of the kids in the red-shirted family, a freckle-faced boy around eight, happened to turn and found himself face-to-face with a crouching Hayley. Her sudden presence shocked him into silence for a moment.

"Hello, what's your name?" Hayley said, offering the kid a warm smile.

It didn't work.

His eyes popped open and he pointed in Hayley's face. "Stranger danger! Stranger danger!"

The red-shirted mother whipped around at her boy's cries to see Hayley on her knees, trying to quiet her kid. "What are you doing? Get away from my son!"

All heads in the bowling alley now turned in

Hayley's direction. Hayley sprung to her feet and quickly walked across one of the lanes, turning her head to one side, to avoid being spotted by Gemma and her druggie friends.

Her head was turned so far she was unable to see where she was going.

"Look out!" a man yelled.

Hayley spun around to see Reverend Staples frantically waving his arms in the air at her.

Hayley suddenly realized she was in the middle of a bowling lane and Reverend Staples's bowling ball was barreling straight for her. She broke into a run to avoid getting mowed down by the ball, but she wasn't fast enough. The ball slammed into her right ankle and she fell face-first into the bowling pins.

They scattered in every direction.

She managed to knock down all the remaining pins that were standing.

At least she helped the reverend score a spare.

Reverend Staples and his wife, Edie, hustled down the lane to help Hayley to her feet.

"Are you all right?" Edie asked.

Hayley nodded, forcing a smile. Then she glanced over to see Gemma, who at that moment was staring at her, mouth agape. That's when Hayley noticed the birthday decorations and cake set up in the corner.

Gemma marched over, screaming at the top of her lungs, "*Mom!* What are you doing here?"

"I . . . I didn't recognize the kids you left with, so I—"

"They're Tina's cousins visiting from New Hampshire. We all carpooled to the party," Gemma said evenly, her arms folded.

"Well, don't I feel like the fool," Hayley said, laughing, trying to make light of the situation.

Nobody else laughed.

"I can't believe you embarrassed me like that. Just go home, please."

"Wait just a minute, young lady. What did that boy give you before you came in here? It looked like some kind of pill. Are you high?"

The big kid who was driving pulled something out of his pocket and handed it to Hayley. "You mean these?"

It was a can of Altoids mints.

"We shared a bag of Funyuns on the way up here, so we had stinky breath," Gemma said, seething.

"Want one?" the boy offered Hayley.

"No, thank you. I'm fine," Hayley said, barely audible.

Hayley looked over to Mona and Liddy for support, but they had already quickly downed their beers at the bar and were slinking toward the exit before Gemma spotted them too.

Hayley feared she had just crossed a line and perhaps lost her daughter's trust for good.

Chapter 11

"I'm really not comfortable appearing on camera, Bessie," Hayley said.

"Nonsense. You're a natural," Bessie said, fluffing her own hair as she stared into a mirror.

A pimply kid around Dustin's age, wearing a Jay-Z t-shirt and tattered jeans, stood behind a mounted camera. Next to him was a pudgy kid holding a cheap-looking boom mike.

"Where did you get all this equipment?" Hayley asked.

"Rented it from the high school. My crew members are volunteers from the visual-arts department. They're getting extra credit for helping me out."

Bessie had decided to make a promo video for her burgeoning candy business and post it on YouTube. When she called Hayley to come over to her house, Hayley just assumed the special candy she promised to whip up for her was ready to be picked up.

But it wasn't.

Bessie had other plans.

She needed a straight man for her video. Since Bessie had very few friends, Hayley was basically her first and only choice.

"What do you want me to do?" Hayley asked.

"Just be yourself. You'll be my guest. After all, you're somewhat of a local celebrity with your cooking column. Now don't worry. You can just stand here and smile and I'll do all the talking."

"Like a *Price Is Right* model."

"Exactly," Bessie said as she finished primping. That didn't seem so bad.

"Okay, let's try one and see what we get," Bessie said. "You boys ready?"

They nodded, but they seemed noncommittal. The plump one yawned.

"Okay, we're rolling. . . . Sound is speeding . . . and action!" the pimply kid said.

Bessie smiled brightly and looked straight into the camera. "Hello, everyone, I'm Bessie, your favorite chocolatier. Today I have a special guest here with me. I've invited my dear friend, Hayley Powell, over because I'm dying for her to try some of my delicious chocolate candies you can buy online at my website, BessiesSweetTreats.com. Go ahead, Hayley. Have one."

Bessie waved a lumpy-looking chocolate in front of Hayley's face.

Hayley didn't expect a taste test.

But she went with it.

Hayley bit into the chocolate. It didn't taste as bad as she had expected.

"Hmmmm . . . so good, Bessie. Yummy," Hayley said stiffly. Her acting talents were never going to make Meryl Streep nervous.

"How would you describe the filling?" Bessie said to Hayley, but the chocolatier was still looking straight into the camera.

"Is that almond?" Hayley guessed.

"No, it's walnut. Cut!"

Bessie looked at Hayley disappointed. "I guess we should have rehearsed first. Let's try another take."

This time Hayley was prepared to guess the correct ingredients; but every time she thought they were done, Bessie insisted on doing another take. She wanted her inaugural video to be absolutely perfect.

Which meant after twenty-four more takes, Hayley had eaten a full box of chocolates.

Hayley's stomach was churning.

She felt queasy.

And she actually felt dizzy from the sugar high.

"Just one more, Hayley. For safety."

"Safety? We've done it two dozen times."

"I know. But on that last one, you winced as you

ate my chocolate. I can't have you wincing, Hayley. People will get the wrong idea."

"I winced because I can't eat any more. I just can't, Bessie. I'm about to be sick," Hayley pleaded.

Bessie just pouted and shook her head as if Hayley were being a kitchen diva.

"I'm sorry . . . I just . . ." Hayley stopped herself. She knew in her gut Bessie was never going to take no for an answer.

Bessie gave her the puppy dog eyes. "Just one more? For me?"

Hayley found herself nodding.

Bessie clapped her hands excitedly and turned to her crew members, who were texting. Her smile faded in an instant. "Focus, you imbeciles, or I tell your teacher you goofed off the whole time and you'll get no credit!"

The boys snapped to attention; one hit a button on the camera and the other lifted up the boom mike.

Hayley went through the motions while Bessie encouraged her to try her chocolate, and Hayley made sure to keep a smile pasted on her face and tried desperately not to wince as she ate the chocolate. She thought she was doing pretty well at pretending to be over the moon for the chocolate as she chewed and chewed. This one was loaded with sticky caramel.

She felt an odd texture on her tongue.

It wasn't gooey.

It was something stringy.

What the hell was that?

It was like . . . hair!

Or cat fur!

Oh, Lord, no!

Supermarket Ron was right.

Bessie's unsanitary kitchen had led to this!

She was eating cat fur!

Hayley gagged, reaching into her mouth with her fingers to try and pull it out.

Bessie never took her eyes off the camera. "Hayley, are you okay?"

Hayley shook her head and then, without warning, she felt bile rising up in her throat. She tried in vain to swallow it, but it was too overwhelming and powerful.

She vomited all over the place.

Bessie screamed.

The pimply kid behind the camera burst out laughing.

The plump one turned green at the horrific sight, dropped his boom mike, and threw up a torrent of liquid goo himself.

Bessie just screamed, "Shut the camera off! Shut it off now!"

Hayley wiped her mouth with her sleeve and just apologized over and over again to poor Bessie, who was nearly catatonic from the shock of Hayley spitting up her delicious chocolates in such a violent manner.

To make matters worse, Bessie's cats appeared out of nowhere and began rubbing up against Hayley's leg. Two more jumped up on the island counter and licked a bowl dripping with chocolate. All those cats closing in on her, like a scene from some frightful Stephen King horror novel, made her feel even sicker.

Bessie finally snapped out of her stunned state and hastily grabbed a mop and a pail and began madly scrubbing the floors clean.

The cats just kept on coming, and Hayley couldn't stop herself from thinking about the fur in the chocolates.

She had to get out of there before she got sick again.

Bessie collapsed in tears, resting her forehead on the mop handle.

Hayley signaled to the two boys to give them some privacy. They appeared grateful and high-tailed it out of there.

"Bessie, I'm sorry. But it was only one take. We got a bunch of good ones you can use on YouTube."

"I just wanted my video to be perfect and show that awful Nina Foster-Jones she's not the only game in town."

Nina Foster-Jones was a local caterer, very snooty, who gained a reputation with the wealthy summer crowd for her offbeat hors d'oeuvres and her scrumptious desserts. However, during the winter months when most of her clients had left town and business was slow, she worked part-time at an insurance company.

"Why do you care about her?" Hayley gently asked.

"Because she thinks I'm stealing her ideas."

"What ideas?"

"Starting a candy business, like she did with those fancy desserts of hers, and doing videos for YouTube, like she did, and calling my new business Bessie's Sweet Treats."

"Why? What does she call her company?"

"Nina's Sweet Treats."

"Oh."

"It's not like people are going to confuse the two. I'm Bessie. She's Nina. Duh!"

Hayley was in no mood to argue with Bessie, even though it did seem Nina had a point.

"I'm collecting enemies left and right. First Ron at the Shop 'n Save, then that doofus, Cody, at the bank, and Wolf, my obnoxious ex. Then yesterday when I was at the high school renting the equipment, Nina happened to be there because one of her hellions was in trouble again. She saw me and just started yelling at me and warning me to stop stealing her ideas, or else. . . ."

"Or else what?"

"Or else she'd kill me."

"She didn't really say that."

"Yes, she did. Twice. She would've said it a third time, but I elbowed her in the throat."

"You did what?"

"She deserved it."

"Did she call the police?"

"She was going to, but Principal Harkins didn't want a scandal at the school. He offered to let Nina's punk kid off the hook if she just left quietly and forgot all about it."

"Bessie, you really need to control your temper. You can't go around hitting people."

"Nina Foster-Jones is a Rachael Ray wannabe no-talent and I'm not going to allow her to intimidate me. If she wants to try and kill me, I say bring it!"

Chapter 12

The following Monday, Gemma was still not speaking to Hayley after the Beer 'n Bowl birthday party debacle, so Hayley decided to give her daughter some space. She was not about to give up on finding the root of her daughter's problem; but for now, she felt it best to let Gemma cool off. After all, it wasn't her most shining moment crashing Reverend Staples's private event for his daughter, family, and friends. Her history with the kind minister was a checkered one, to be sure.

Gemma skipped dinner and went straight to her room, mumbling something about having a lot of homework. Hayley didn't believe her, but let it go. Dustin lay on the couch, watching the Disney Channel show *Jessie* and chuckling, while Leroy slept soundly on Dustin's stomach, rising up and down with the belly laughs. Blueberry, meanwhile, sat perched underneath the coffee table. His beady yellow eyes stared at anyone who dared walk past.

Hayley sat in the recliner, with her laptop in front of her. She was trying to write her own column after spending so much time trying to finish Bruce's. She was struggling for a topic. Chocolate, of course, was on her mind constantly. Maybe a nice mole sauce. At least it wasn't candy. The thought of candy was still making her nauseous.

Her cell phone, which rested on the arm of the recliner, lit up and buzzed. Hayley checked the screen. It was Bessie. She debated whether or not she should answer it. Guilt got the best of her.

"Hi, Bessie!"

"Good news, girlfriend! Your special chocolates are ready for you to pick up."

Hayley choked, fighting back the urge to vomit again.

"I think Hayley's Kisses are going to be a huge seller, but I'll let you be the judge," Bessie said.

"Thanks, Bessie. I'll swing by after work tomorrow to pick them up."

"Oh," Bessie said, disappointed.

"I've just had my fill of chocolates for one day."

"No, I understand. I'm sorry about that. That was me being the Type A perfectionist. I never should've made you eat that many chocolates. I told the boys to make sure they erase that take so it never gets out."

Hayley wasn't sure she was going to trust two

teenage boys to follow Bessie's explicit instructions, but she was not going to worry about that now.

"So I'll see you tomorrow?" Hayley asked.

No response.

Just dead air.

"Bessie?"

Hayley heard faint wheezing.

Then there was a *click*.

Did she hang up?

No. There was heavy breathing.

Bessie had dropped the phone.

Suddenly she had a sickening feeling in her gut.

And it wasn't her overdose from chocolates.

"Bessie? Bessie?"

Hayley jumped out of the recliner, her phone still pressed to her ear. "I'll be back, Dustin!"

"Where are you going?" he asked, eyes glued to the TV.

"Bessie's. I may be awhile!"

Blueberry hissed as she raced past the coffee table.

Hayley grabbed the car keys off the kitchen counter, jumped in her car, and raced over to Bessie's house.

All the lights were on in the house.

Bessie's car was parked in the driveway.

Hayley raced to the door and rang the bell.

No answer.

She rang again.

Still, nothing.

She tried the doorknob.

It was unlocked.

She poked her head inside. "Bessie? It's me, Hayley. You got me a little worried. Are you okay?"

Hayley walked into the kitchen.

There was a bubbling pot of chocolate on the stove. Some of it was spraying onto the kitchen counter, so Hayley shut off the burner.

A cat jumped up on the counter next to her and began purring.

Another was rubbing up against her leg again.

There was a lot of meowing.

Everywhere Hayley looked, she saw another cat. "Bessie?"

Hayley left the kitchen and walked into the living room.

More cats.

About seven.

And they were all gathered around a body on the floor. Two were licking the face. One was perched on top of the stomach. A few more nestled between the legs.

Hayley instantly recognized the Garfield tattoo on the neck.

It was Bessie.

The phone was still in her hand.

She was dead.

Surrounded by cats.

Two dozen chocolates wrapped in pink cellophane were scattered about the floor.

Island Food & Spirits
by
Hayley Powell

A recent unexpected trip to the Beer 'n Bowl in Ellsworth reminded me of the dramatic events that unfolded last year when my girls' night out with my friends Mona and Liddy led us to that popular Friday-night local hot spot. The three of us were looking forward to a fun, laid-back evening with some ice-cold beer and amateur bowling, but things didn't quite work out that way.

Right off the bat, Liddy got into a heated argument with the gentleman in charge of renting out the bowling shoes. She flatly told him that she was going to wear her new Jimmy Choo leather flats to bowl in, because no fashion-conscious patron such as herself would be caught dead wearing the hideous yellow-and-red bowling shoes he held up in front of her. The man informed Liddy she was welcome to wear her own shoes—as long as she wore them out the same door she came in.

Being the peacemaker of the trio, I quickly stepped in and reminded Liddy that this bowling alley actually had a bar that served Cosmopolitans, which might help make those god-awful shoes a little less offensive. Liddy grimaced, but she finally agreed and snatched the bowling shoes out of the man's hands and stalked off.

As we laced up our shoes, we noticed the place was packed with mostly women bowlers. Then it dawned on us it was Ladies' League Night. Just what we didn't need! None of us had bowled in years, and we were about to look foolish in front of a bunch of competitive near professionals. If only it had been Bumper Bowling Day for Kids, then perhaps we would've at least stood a chance.

After a rusty start, we actually began avoiding the gutter and knocking a few pins down with each turn. The Cosmos were emboldening us and building our confidence.

We worked up quite an appetite, so Mona fetched us the most amazing chicken burritos with a mouthwatering spicy mole sauce. It was so good she and I ordered extra cups of it to dip our burritos into. Who knew bowling alley food was this good?

Meanwhile, Liddy refused to eat, because she was on yet another one of her diets. None of her diets, of course, ever seemed to forbid alcohol. And on an empty stomach, after four Cosmos, she was getting downright belligerent. We decided to get her out of there before she caused a scene; but sadly, we weren't fast enough. When one female bowler yelled at Liddy for walking in front of her while she was trying to bowl and her ball ended up in the gutter, Liddy slurred an insult about the the loud, obnoxious Hawaiian bowling shirt the woman was wearing. Unfortunately, all the women on the team were wearing the same team shirt and were also the size of sumo wrestlers. The last thing we needed was a brawl at the Beer 'n Bowl. What kind of example would that be to my kids?

I didn't see what happened next, but more insults were exchanged. Liddy's spicy mole sauce somehow ended up on half the team's Hawaiian shirts; and before Mona and I could react, there was a stampede of angry, big-boned bowlers heading straight for us!

Mona yelled, "Run!" and the three of us hightailed it out of there. We jumped into Mona's truck and sped off into the night toward the island, leaving seven women bowlers chasing after us, throwing their cups of beer at Mona's taillights.

We were stunned into silence as we drove home, and none of us spoke for at least ten minutes. But as we crossed over the Trenton Bridge, Liddy let out a blood-curdling scream, which nearly caused Mona to drive off the bridge into the icy, dark water below. Liddy was pointing at her feet. She was still wearing those ugly yellow-and-red bowling shoes. Mona and I couldn't help ourselves. We burst into a fit of giggles. Liddy didn't see the humor. How was she ever going to retrieve her brand-new five-hundred-dollar Jimmy Choo leather flats?

Mona informed Liddy there was no way we were turning around and risking our lives and that she was perfectly willing to sacrifice her ten-dollar Ked sneakers she scored at Marden's last year. I agreed with her, since I had bought myself the same pair.

When Mona and Liddy dropped me off, my mind was already racing to whip up my own version of the Beer 'n Bowl's spicy mole sauce, which had tasted so good before our abrupt departure. So in keeping with our chocolate theme, here it is. But let's first start the evening off with a yummy cocktail recipe, since it's never fun to cook when you're thirsty.

With a good mole sauce to put on your shredded, grilled, or baked chicken or beef, nothing tastes as good with it than a nice cold pitcher of Mexican beer margaritas! Olé!

Mexican Beer Margaritas

<u>Ingredients</u>
1 (12 ounce) can frozen limeade
1½ cups (12 ounces) gold tequila
12 ounces water
12 ounces Mexican beer or a
    beer of your choice
Ice
1 lime, cut into wedges

In a large pitcher mix together the limeade, tequila, water, and beer and stir well until the limeade has melted. Add lots of

ice and top with the lime wedges.
Add more water if needed.

Hayley's Spicy Mole Sauce

Ingredients
4½ cups chicken broth
3 tablespoons olive oil
1 cup onion, finely chopped
3 tablespoons fresh garlic, chopped
1 teaspoon dried oregano
1 teaspoon ground cumin
¼ teaspoon cinnamon
2½ tablespoons chili powder
3 tablespoons all-purpose flour
2 ounces your favorite dark chocolate, chopped

Heat oil in a large saucepan over medium heat. Add the onion, garlic, oregano, cumin, and cinnamon. Cover and cook until onion is almost tender, stirring occasionally for about 10 minutes.

Mix in the chili powder and flour, stirring for 3 minutes. Gradually whisk in the chicken broth. Increase your heat to medium high. Boil until reduced, about 35 minutes, stirring occasionally. Remove from heat and whisk in the chocolate; season with salt and pepper, if desired.

Chapter 13

Hayley couldn't believe what Sal was telling her. "She said what?"

"She's not doing an autopsy," Sal said, before struggling into his army green winter parka and pulling a red wool cap over his balding head. "You want to grab a burger and onion rings at Jordan's with me?"

"I was going to spend my lunch hour writing Bruce's column about Bessie Winthrop's death."

"Why? It's not a crime."

"Well, we don't know that. And now we never will, since the county coroner refuses to do an autopsy on her," Hayley said.

Sal shook his head. "Bessie died of natural causes. Sabrina is certain of it."

Sabrina Merryweather was the county coroner—not to mention the mean girl who tortured Hayley all through high school. In recent years Sabrina had forgotten all about her abhorrent behavior toward Hayley when they were teenagers. Now she considered Hayley to be one of her closest friends. Hayley went along with the charade because every corpse in town eventually wound up on Sabrina's examining table, and Sabrina was a font of information whenever circumstances forced Hayley to investigate a local dead body independently. Hayley was fast gaining a reputation around town not only as an amateur chef, but also as Bar Harbor's very own Miss Marple.

"So, are you coming or what?" Sal asked. There was a gruff tone to his voice that Hayley chalked up to hunger, since she could hear his stomach growling clear across the room.

"No, I'm going to hang out here and get some work done."

Sal pointed to a white box, with a pink ribbon tied around it, which was sitting on top of her desk. They were the special chocolates Bessie had made for her right before she died. After Police Chief Sergio Alvares conducted a thorough sweep through the whole house and determined Bessie's death was not a homicide, he allowed Hayley to take the box home with her. She didn't want them. She was never going to eat another piece of chocolate as long as she lived. But she also didn't want to appear ungrateful and callous; after all, Bessie had put her heart and soul into making those chocolates, and the least she could do was graciously accept them.

"Well, don't eat too many of those. I don't want to hear you whining all afternoon about how you need to eat more healthy after you finish the whole box."

"Says the man who is on his way out for a burger, with everything on it, and fried onion rings."

"Don't tell my wife. I have to load up at lunchtime because she's got me on this cockamamie diet. She's force-feeding me every lousy night a crappy piece of salmon and a tiny, little side salad that wouldn't satisfy a blue jay. My life sucks!"

Sal blew out the door.

The second he was gone, Hayley picked up the phone and called Sabrina Merryweather at her office.

"Hey, girlfriend!" Sabrina chirped, picking up on the first ring. "I saw it was the *Island Times* on my caller ID, so I knew it was my bestie checking up on me. When are we having a girls' night with you, me, and Liddy?"

Sabrina knew not to include Mona, since Mona was the type to say what she was thinking, and had told Sabrina on multiple social occasions exactly what she thought of Sabrina. Much of it involved four-letter words.

"I miss you!" Sabrina cooed. "You never call me!"

Hayley mentally envisioned Sabrina making her cute, pouty face that got her lots of dates with football players in high school and straight A's from most of the male teachers. It was still highly effective.

Just not with Hayley.

"I'm calling you now."

"You want something. I can always tell," Sabrina said, sighing.

"What kind of friend would I be if I only called when I wanted something?"

"So you're just calling to say hi?" Sabrina asked suspiciously.

"Yes. I want to hear all about what's going on with you."

"Well, my husband's away at some artists' colony, which I'm paying for, of course, and, frankly, I couldn't be happier. I've just been going home after work at night, pouring myself a glass of wine, and taking a bubble bath. It's been sheer heaven. I'm going through brochures now, trying to find an even longer artists' retreat—say in Hawaii— which lasts something like three weeks that I can send him away to next month. What about you?"

"My daughter's not speaking to me. I'm overwhelmed at work writing two separate columns. . . ." Hayley paused for maximum effect. "Then there's the death of my dear friend Bessie Winthrop."

"I didn't know you were friends with her."

"Yes, Bessie and I have gotten very close the past couple of weeks."

"Really? That's surprising. I can't picture you two together."

But she could picture Hayley being *her* close friend. Even after Sabrina had spread vicious, false rumors senior year about Hayley having been impregnated by the janitor's slow assistant—a guy with bug eyes and a constantly runny nose. Sabrina certainly had no trouble picturing that.

Hayley tried to keep her emotions in check. Sabrina was right. She did need something, and she wasn't about to blow her chance to get it.

Hayley proceeded with caution. "I suppose you heard that I was the one who found the body."

"Honey pie, don't you stumble across *every* dead body in town? I mean, let's face it, girl, this is becoming a huge pattern."

"I just can't believe she's gone."

"I can," Sabrina said, snorting. "She was a walking time bomb."

"She may have been a little overweight, but—"

"A little? Hayley, she was at least a hundred pounds overweight! And I'm looking at her medical charts right now. She had untreated high blood pressure, was prediabetic, and had a massive blockage in her arteries. It's no wonder she keeled over. Frankly, I'm shocked it didn't happen sooner."

"Is that why you're not going to perform an autopsy?"

"How did you know that?"

"Sal told me."

There was a long pause.

"Sabrina, you still there?"

"I knew you were just calling to get the 411 on Bessie," Sabrina said.

"No, that's not true," Hayley lied. "In fact, I was calling to find out when you were free for that drink."

"Really?" Sabrina said, totally unconvinced.

"Yes. I swear on the life of Mark Harmon, and you know how much I love him!"

"Wow! You really are serious," Sabrina said, giggling.

Hayley felt it was safer not to mention that although she still adored Mark Harmon, she was currently lusting after LL Cool J, the rapper with all those muscles, who starred on that other *NCIS* show that followed sexy Mark's.

"Okay," Sabrina said. "I'm free tomorrow night."

"Tomorrow?"

Hayley wasn't sure she was up to seeing Sabrina that soon.

"Yes, Hayley, tomorrow. I'm waiting for an answer. Are you serious about wanting to spend some quality time together?"

Hayley was boxed into a corner.

She had to commit.

"Yes. Absolutely. Let's say seven-thirty. My brother Randy's bar."

"Done. And don't you even *think* about canceling."

Sabrina hung up.

Hayley groaned to herself.

A drink with Sabrina.

She'd rather be undergoing a root canal.

But it was for the good of the cause.

Still, the thought of a girls' night out with Sabrina was very stressful. And stress always made Hayley ravenous. She had to eat something pronto. But the only food around was Bessie's box of chocolates.

Damn.

She should've gone with Sal for that burger when she had the chance.

Hayley found herself unwrapping the pink ribbon from around the box and perusing the selection inside. She picked one up, examined it, made sure there wasn't any cat hair sticking out of it, and ate it.

It melted in her mouth.

And no taste of fur.

Hallelujah.

She ate another one.

These candies were delectably delicious.

Hayley could see these actually selling.

Big-time.

A wave of sadness washed over her. Bessie had

finally concocted a winning recipe—one that would have undoubtedly put her on the map. Now she was never going to live to see it.

Sadness also made Hayley hungry.

So she kept diving into the box of chocolates.

As she bit into the fifth one, her luck ran out.

There was something inside it.

But it wasn't cat hair.

It was harder.

Like chewing paper.

Hayley pulled it out of her mouth. She was right. It was a small, crumpled-up piece of paper that had been stuffed inside the candy.

She set it down on her desk and flattened it out.

Hayley gasped.

Scrawled on the piece of paper in pen were the words *I think someone is trying to kill me.*

Chapter 14

Hayley knew the note was meant for her. Bessie had made that box of Hayley's Kisses especially for her. That's why she was so anxious for Hayley to pick them up.

But why?

Why couldn't she just tell her about her suspicion?

Was she afraid her phone was bugged?

Or someone was watching her?

And who would want to murder Bessie?

On second thought, was there anyone in town who *didn't* want to murder Bessie?

Sergio was done with his investigation.

Natural causes.

Sabrina was finished with her findings.

Natural causes.

Even if Hayley showed up at both their offices with the small scrap of paper she nearly chewed up and swallowed, it wouldn't be enough to change their minds.

No.

This was something Hayley was going to have to pursue on her own.

Again.

And she could start by going over to Bessie's house and searching for clues. Maybe Bessie left another note, some kind of sign, anything that might indicate who might have gone to such desperate measures to get rid of her.

And just how did he or she do it?

Sabrina was snotty and two-faced, but she was pretty damn good at her job. Hayley did not doubt for a second that Bessie was battling a multitude of health problems. But with no autopsy, then whatever method the killer might have used would be buried with Bessie forever.

And someone in Bessie's life would be getting away with murder.

Hayley reached into her bag and rummaged around, finally finding the key to Bessie's house, which Bessie had given her. She knew Sal would be gone for at least another forty-five minutes. Bessie's house was just a few blocks away from the office.

Hayley sprung to her feet, grabbed her coat, and hurried out the door.

When she arrived at Bessie's house and let herself in, using the key, she was once again overcome by the stench of kitty litter. The only difference was there were no mangy cats roaming about. She had heard through Randy, who was told by his partner, Sergio, that all the cats had been removed and were currently at the handsome, new vet Dr. Palmer's office being medically treated before, hopefully, being put up for adoption. Dr. Aaron Palmer.

What a kind, sweet, giving man.

And so good-looking.

His wife was a very lucky woman.

Hayley stopped herself.

She wasn't here to moon over Aaron.

Or Dr. Palmer.

She wasn't that familiar with him to be on a first-name basis.

She was here to look for anything that might suggest Bessie's death was not from natural causes.

Hayley started with the drawers in the kitchen, opening one to find a tray of rusty, smudged old utensils, another one to find the last remnants of some spare plastic wrap and tinfoil. She moved to another row and the top one was some kind of mail drawer stuffed with unpaid parking tickets, unopened bills, legal documents, and paperwork. She quickly fanned through the stack, her eyes focusing on a piece of paper issued by the local court. It was a restraining order taken out against one of Bessie's ex-boyfriends, Wolf Conway. Well, that wasn't a surprise. He was the size of a Mack truck and very intimidating. And he sure didn't seem to like Bessie very much.

A red folder caught her eye. She flipped it open and perused the contents. It was from the office of Ted Rivers, a local lawyer whose office was upstairs from Liddy's real estate firm. Hayley skimmed the document. It appeared Bessie was embroiled in a lawsuit with her neighbors Mark and Mary Garber. Hayley knew them casually. They had moved to Bar Harbor from Rhode Island after visiting Bar Harbor one summer and falling in love with the island and its lifestyle. Hayley folded up the paper and slid it into the pocket of her jeans and continued her search.

Hayley walked up the creaky stairs to Bessie's bedroom. Dirty, wrinkled clothes were strewn about. A wall mirror above the dresser was so smudged that Hayley couldn't even see her own reflection. There was makeup powder everywhere; cans of hair spray were on the floor; the bed was smelly and unmade. Hayley didn't need to eat a lot of chocolate to feel nauseous again.

She glanced at a digital camera lying next to a Garfield lamp on a side table next to the bed. Bessie certainly was a big fan of the cartoon cat. She picked up the camera, switched it on, and started scrolling through the photos. Hayley was shocked to discover about twenty-five pictures of Cody Donovan, the loan officer from the bank, in bed with a woman whose face was hidden in the shadows. She couldn't see the woman's face, but she certainly had shapely legs. And on her wrist was a very distinctive gold poppy bangle, with a polished band of sterling silver. It was right in front of the camera lens because the woman was holding a fistful of Cody's hair as he made love to her. Even though Hayley could not identify her, the woman was most definitely *not* Cody's uptight and jealous wife, Kerry. It looked as if the photos had been taken from outside a first-story bedroom window.

It was obviously Bessie who had taken the photos.

And did Cody know about them?

Hayley was just about finished looking through the photos, and was about to head to the storage closet she had spotted just down the hall from the bedroom, when suddenly she heard a creaking sound.

And then another.

Someone was coming up the stairs.

Slowly.

Hayley stood frozen in place.

She held her breath.

Creak.

The intruder continued his ascent.

Faster now.

Like he was charging toward her.

Hayley dropped the camera on the floor and scooted into the bathroom, quietly closing the door and looking around. There was no window to slip out, nowhere to go. She heard the intruder walking around in the bedroom. It was only a matter of seconds before he came into the bathroom.

Hayley pulled open the medicine cabinet, hoping to find some kind of weapon. If only she had picked up the can of hair spray in the other room, the aerosol would have made a decent pepper spray if she got him directly in the eyes.

The door handle to the bathroom jiggled. Hayley climbed into the bathtub and closed the curtain. She pressed herself up against the tile wall as the door banged open and someone entered.

She heard heavy breathing.

God, what a way to go.

What if the guy had a knife? Like in *Psycho*. She always felt so sorry for Janet Leigh in that movie. Everyone makes a few mistakes in life, but poor Janet's crime was stealing a few lousy bucks from her office and having an affair with a hunky, shirtless stud. Big deal. Did she really have to pay for it with her life at the hands of a crazy, cross-dressing, mother-loving Tony Perkins? Well, Norman Bates. Tony Perkins was probably a very nice person just *playing* a nutcase.

The intruder crossed to the shower.

She could see his outline through the curtain.

Tall.

Broad-shouldered.

Hayley saw the man grab a fistful of the curtain. She squeezed her eyes shut and prayed.

The curtain was flung open and Hayley let out a scream.

"Hayley?"

Hayley popped open one eye.

It wasn't Norman Bates.

It was Sergio. Her brother Randy's partner.

And Bar Harbor's esteemed police chief.

His gun was drawn and he had a grim look on his face.

Hayley decided to make the best of a potentially disastrous situation. She gave him her brightest smile. "Sergio! Now this is a happy coincidence! What are you doing here?"

Sergio didn't return the smile.

At that moment Hayley knew she was in big trouble.

Chapter 15

Randy nervously popped open a bottle of Coppola Merlot and poured three glasses. Hayley was seated on the couch in the living room of the sprawling oceanside New England house that Randy and Sergio shared.

Sergio was stoking the flames in the fireplace with a poker and then turned to Hayley; the poker was aimed at her as if about to impale her.

"You going to use that thing on me?" Hayley asked.

"No. But someone needs to pound some sense into you," Sergio said sternly. But his thick Brazilian accent even made the angriest comment seem sexy.

"I'm sorry," Hayley said. "I wasn't thinking."

Randy balanced three glasses of red wine and set one down on the coffee table in front of Hayley. He sipped from another as he delivered the third one to Sergio, who put the poker back in the cast-iron fireplace-tool stand.

"She's always had a nosy nature. I don't know where she gets that from," Randy said.

Sergio stared at him, the irony not lost on him. "It must run in the family."

"How did you know I was there?" Hayley asked.

"Mary Garber was in her yard replacing one of her storm windows and she saw someone moving around inside Bessie Winthrop's place next door."

"She didn't see that it was just me?"

"No, Hayley, and even if she did, you were breaking and entering. She did the right thing by calling the police."

"Is it technically breaking and entering if the owner of the house is no longer among the living?" Randy asked, trying to be helpful.

Sergio glared at him and Randy took a big gulp of his wine, pretending he hadn't said anything.

"What were you doing there?" Sergio wanted to know.

"Well, since you asked, I am not one hundred percent convinced that Bessie's death was purely from natural causes. You see—"

"I am. I am one hundred percent convinced," Sergio said in a loud voice.

"Okay, well, let me try to change your mind—"

"No," Sergio said, downing his wine. "I'm tired from a really long day and I'm in no mood to hear about your wild, unsusceptible theories."

"Unsusceptible to what?" Hayley asked.

"He means 'unsubstantiated,'" Randy said, again trying to be helpful.

English was not Sergio's first language; on occasion he was known to mix up his words.

"Okay, first of all, I have no theories, just a few clues. But I did hear from Bessie and she believed someone wanted to kill her," Hayley said.

"So she said something to you when she called you last night, right before she died?" Sergio asked.

"No, she didn't say anything to me at that point. It was after that."

"So she mailed you a letter or sent you an e-mail, which you didn't open until after you discovered the body?"

"No, nothing like that. She put a note in a piece of chocolate. I bit into it."

Sergio stared at Hayley for a long moment and then turned and headed for the stairs.

"Good night."

"Sergio, wait . . . ," Hayley pleaded.

Sergio stopped at the foot of the stairs and turned around. "Stop, Hayley. Stop right now. I do not want you making this a 'thing,' like you usually do."

"'Thing'? What do you mean 'thing'? What do I make a *thing*?"

"He means your propensity to poke your nose into affairs that don't concern you," Randy said.

Hayley sipped her wine and pouted.

Just like Sabrina Merryweather.

Maybe if she looked as cute as Sabrina did in high school doing it, she just might get somewhere with Sergio. On second thought Sergio was gay, so it was probably a lost cause.

Besides, he was already halfway up the stairs.

"Case closed," he said before walking into the bedroom and slamming the door.

"Don't worry," Randy said, crossing over to the dining-room table to retrieve the bottle of Merlot. "His hands are tied because the official investigation into the cause of death has been determined. He's done with it. But he knows you won't listen to him, and on some level he's at peace with that."

"What do you mean?"

Randy poured them both another glass, finishing the bottle. "Sergio, in all of his wisdom, once said that when it comes to solving a mystery, you're like a Bieber with a tennis ball."

"I'm confused. I didn't even know Justin Bieber played tennis."

"He meant to say 'beagle.' And his point was, when it comes to finding answers, you're like a beagle with a tennis ball. There's no way you're ever letting it go."

Hayley smiled.

Sergio was a smart man.

And he was absolutely right.

Chapter 16

"My paper is not the *National Enquirer*, Hayley! We deal in facts here," Sal barked as he bulldozed his way into the front office.

"What are you talking about?" Hayley said, averting her eyes, her face reddening.

"You know damn well what I'm talking about. Bruce's crime column. That little piece of fiction you willfully came up with and just e-mailed me!"

Hayley rose from her desk. "I happen to believe everything I wrote is true."

"It reads more like a gossip column, Hayley. It's pure breathless speculation. The facts are, Bessie Winthrop died of a simple heart attack. End of story."

"Well, that's speculation as well, because Sabrina Merryweather refuses to do an autopsy on the body, so we can't be sure."

Sal thrust his chest out like a rooster's. He wasn't used to Hayley standing up to him. "Now you listen here. I'm the boss around here and I decide what gets printed and posted online. I only want stories that deal in facts. So I'm making an executive decision. I'm killing the story."

"Fine. But I think you're being sexist."

Sal's cheeks were now redder than Hayley's.

His round face looked like a ripe apple.

"'Sexist'? *Me*? What the hell are you talking about? I donated to the breast cancer awareness marathon through Acadia National Park last summer. I wore the pink-ribbon pin for a week! My wife works! I have the complete series of *Xena: Warrior Princess* on DVD! How could anybody call me 'sexist'?"

"Because, Sal, Bruce Linney has a long history of fudging facts and teasing his readers with innuendo in order to slant a story in the direction he wants it to go. He's like the male version of Nancy Grace. And never once have you buried one of his columns. Not even the time he went so far as to suggest that I was a cold-blooded killer who was going around poisoning people with my clam chowder!"

Sal opened his mouth to protest, but he stopped himself. He realized he had nothing to say. He just couldn't argue that point. Hayley was right. He did give Bruce a lot of leeway when it came to his column.

It bugged him that Hayley was getting the best of him.

And Hayley knew it.

Sal paused. Gathered his thoughts. Exhaled a breath that turned into a whistle before he spoke. "But we don't know for a certainty that Bessie was murdered. However, you seem to take great pride in insinuating that she was."

"I didn't insinuate anything. I just raised some questions. Sabrina is not bothering with an autopsy. Sergio classified her death as 'from natural causes.' Bessie did have a lot of enemies in town. And I found a note in Bessie's handwriting, hidden inside a chocolate she made especially for me, that clearly said she thought someone wanted to kill her. Those are all cold, hard facts, Sal. Every single one. I am not interested in making anything up."

"Okay, fine. But I'm still not running the story—"

"But, Sal—"

"Hold on. Hear me out. If you do manage to dig up some kind of hard evidence that could reopen the case, then you can write about it to your heart's content."

"So you're letting me investigate on behalf of the paper?"

"Hell no. You do it on your own time. When you're here at the office, I want you writing recipes and covering the real crimes going on in town, like the report I just got that two high-school kids just stole some OxyContin from the pharmacy."

"I'll head over there right now. Thanks, Sal."

"Before you go, where did you hide that bottle of Jack Daniel's whiskey I gave you?"

"The one you told me to keep away from you until after five o'clock?"

"Yeah. What time is it?"

"Ten-thirty. In the morning, FYI."

"Well, you've worn me out a little early, so I think I deserve a pick-me-up."

"You made me promise, Sal."

"What do I have to do to get you to give it to me now?"

"Run my story."

"Anything but that."

Hayley wasn't about to budge.

She reached into her bag, pulled out a key, and set it down on top of her desk.

"What's that?"

"The key to the bottom drawer of the filing cabinet just outside your office. I can take it with me or leave it right here when I go to the pharmacy."

"So the booze is in there?"

Hayley nodded. "Your choice."

"Your friend Sabrina is not going to like it. Your column makes her look incompetent."

"She's not really my friend. I'll risk it."

Sal tried to hold out a bit longer, but it was no use. He lunged toward Hayley's desk and snatched up the key with his chubby fingers. "I'll run the damn story. But no more calling me sexist!"

He hustled into the back of the office faster than Hayley had ever seen him move.

Hayley smiled, satisfied.

She had been given the green light to keep investigating.

And, hopefully, prove everyone wrong.

She felt confident in her mind that Bessie's death had nothing to do with her health.

Bessie Winthrop had been murdered.

Chapter 17

"I have such good news!" Liddy hollered as she burst through the back door and into the kitchen to find Hayley on her hands and knees sopping up cat urine from the hardwood floor in the hallway leading to the living room.

"I sure could use some right about now," Hayley said, giving an icy stare to Blueberry, who squatted on the recliner, flapping his massively thick tail methodically up and down.

"You spill your cocktail?" Liddy asked sympathetically.

"I never had time to make one. Blueberry's been busy all day marking his territory."

"Where's Leroy?"

"Wherever Blueberry isn't."

"I don't know why you agreed to take in that demonic beast. He's just making your life miserable."

"You know I've always been a bleeding heart."

"Yes, but that cat isn't even grateful. Look at him perched on his throne like some spoiled king, as if it's his birthright to be here."

"I'm hoping he's just misunderstood."

"And I'm hoping when I get home I find Channing Tatum in my shower. They're both unattainable fantasies."

Hayley finished wiping the floor and climbed to her feet. "So, what's your news?"

"Well, I happen to know for a fact that you are right."

"About Bessie being murdered?"

"No. I don't care about that. I couldn't stand Bessie. She always made me so nervous. I hate it when I don't know what people are going to say next."

"So, what am I right about?"

"That handsome, new vet is definitely married."

"I thought you said you had good news."

"I do. He's married, but he is separated and filing for divorce. That's a big reason why Dr. Palmer moved here—to make a fresh start."

"How do you know all this?" Hayley asked, mixing herself and Liddy a Jack and Coke. She had whiskey on her mind all afternoon after she gave up the bottle in the drawer to Sal.

"Well, my other good news is I've been dating someone new. A lawyer."

"Ted Rivers, who has an office above yours? He's married, Liddy!"

"I'm not talking about Ted Rivers! I could never sleep with him. I saw him without his shirt on doing crunches at the gym once. He's got so many pimples on his back that it looks like the surface of Mars. Can you imagine running your hands on that? Yuck."

Hayley handed Liddy her cocktail, and Liddy took a generous sip.

"Yummy. You sure do know how to make a cocktail, girlfriend. Anyway, I'm dating Ted's new big rival, Sonny Lipton. Just finished law school last year and opened up a practice in town. Ted's beside himself. He's never had any serious competition before."

"Liddy, Sonny Lipton is something like twenty-five years old."

"Twenty-six, to be precise. And it's wonderful. After that young bartender at the Beer 'n Bowl hit on me last Friday night, I decided to embrace my inner cougar. I picked him up in the produce section of the Shop 'n Save the next day. He was squeezing melons. I was buying bananas. It was all the imagery we needed to see before introducing ourselves and making a date for that night."

"So he told you Aaron's filing for divorce?"

"Oh, is it Aaron already?"

"I mean Dr. Palmer."

"Yes, Sonny's handling it for him. He needed a new lawyer because his wife is using his previous attorney. Sonny loves pillow talk."

"Okay, you really don't need to give me any more details about you and Sonny. So, what am I supposed to do with this information?"

Liddy thought about this for a moment and then broke into a smile. She marched into the living room and pointed to Blueberry. "Your cat clearly has a bladder issue. He's peeing all over the house. You need to take him to the vet for a thorough examination."

"I don't think it's a medical condition. I think it's more of a test of wills. He wants to see what it's going to take to make me crack."

Liddy's finger pointing got a bit too close to Blueberry's face and he lashed out with his claws and slashed the tip of Liddy's index finger, drawing blood. Liddy howled in pain, retracting her finger to her chest as Blueberry hissed at her.

"Why, you fat, furry force of evil! Mess with me again and I'll dump you in a potato sack and drop you right off the Trenton Bridge!"

"Liddy, he doesn't understand a word you're saying."

"No, he understands every word. And I don't think he's ever going to rest until we're all dead," Liddy said, sucking the blood off her finger. "I'm going upstairs for a Band-Aid."

"I don't feel comfortable using Blueberry as an excuse just to show up at Dr. Palmer's office again."

Liddy stopped halfway up the stairs. "Do what you want, Hayley. But there are a lot of single women and divorcées who have their eye on any new man in town who doesn't smell of salt water and gutted fish. I'm just saying, snooze and you lose."

Liddy, of course, was right.

But Hayley had vowed never to be one of those opportunistic, desperate women who sought out a man like it was some sort of competition.

And it seemed a little sad and pathetic to use an obviously disturbed animal as a way to get close to him again.

No.

Absolutely not.

She would not stoop to such tactics.

Still, she couldn't shake the image of those dreamy green bedroom eyes.

Blueberry jumped down off the recliner, marched right back to where Hayley had just cleaned up the cat urine, and peed again. All the while he kept one eye on Hayley, his whiskers lifting upward as he formed an insidious smile on his face.

On second thought, Hayley considered, maybe Dr. Palmer might actually have something to help Blueberry stop peeing so much.

Or just something to calm him down.

Or better yet, something to knock him into a kitty coma.

For years to come.

Chapter 18

"I'm sorry, Dr. Palmer is out of the office right now. How can I help you?" Marla, the vet's assistant, said. She was wearing a pink smock, with blue Smurf characters all over it. She put down her *People* magazine on top of a whole stack that included such gossipy rags as *US, In Touch,* and *Star.*

"You may remember he treated my dog, Leroy, and now I'm hoping he might be able to help me with my cat. Well, he's not really *my* cat. I'm just looking after him until we can find him a permanent home. Actually, it's an interesting story. . . ."

Marla did not seem the least bit interested in hearing Hayley's interesting story, so Hayley just lifted up the pet carrier she was holding and set it down on the desk.

Marla peeked through the cage door. "Who do we have here?"

"Don't get too close. He's a mean one. Hates everybody. I don't want you getting scratched."

Surprisingly, Blueberry wasn't hissing. He just sat in the carrier; his fat, furry body took up most of the space.

"What's his name?"

"Blueberry."

"Hello, Blueberry. I'm Marla," she said, sticking a finger through the metal wire and petting the cat's wet nose.

"No, don't! I'm warning you, he's dangerous and unpredictable!"

But Blueberry didn't go on the attack.

Instead, he stuck his sandpaper-like tongue out and licked Marla's finger.

And he wasn't hissing.

He was purring.

Yes, purring!

A sound Hayley had never heard come out of him.

The sign of a contented cat.

This was unbelievable.

"He doesn't seem so bad," Marla said, pressing her face up against the cage door and pursing her lips to make a series of kissing sounds.

Hayley stood in front of her, flabbergasted. Then she poked her head around to check the carrier and see if she had accidentally brought the wrong cat.

No, it was definitely Blueberry.

Purring and licking.

Like a normal cat.

Hayley was starting to suspect this was all a plot by Blueberry to make her look crazy.

He was *that* diabolical.

Marla unlatched the door and reached in to pull Blueberry out. She held him close to her bosom and gently stroked his back.

Hayley's mouth just hung open.

Blueberry rubbed his face against Marla's chest. The purring was almost deafening.

"You certainly have a way with animals," Hayley said, still not quite believing her eyes.

"I know. I thought about being a vet when I was a kid. For about half a minute. What I really want to do is to move to Hollywood and become an actress. I did high-school plays, so I know I have the talent."

"Well, good luck."

"I don't need luck. I know it's going to happen. I'm going to star in big movies and marry a famous actor or maybe just a handsome professional, like Dr. Palmer."

There was a gleam in her eye when she spoke of the good doctor.

Hayley wasn't the only one who had a slight crush on the new vet in town.

"Will the doctor be back soon?" Hayley asked.

Still cradling Blueberry, Marla leaned forward in her chair and clicked a button on her computer bringing up Dr. Palmer's calendar.

"I keep track of his schedule, so I know where

he is at all times," Marla said with a self-satisfied smile, almost bragging. Marla clearly liked to think of herself as the most important woman in the doctor's life now that he was divorcing his wife.

At least until she moved to Hollywood and married Ryan Gosling.

Blueberry was now on his back in Marla's arms like a newborn baby, looking euphoric as she scratched his belly. She was scanning the calendar on her computer screen.

"He won't be back in the office until tomorrow morning around seven. I can put you in the book if you'd like to come back."

"Does that mean I have to attempt to put Blueberry back in the carrier? He's not very cooperative."

Marla stood up from her desk and effortlessly set Blueberry down in the carrier and shut the door, locking the latch again.

"I . . . I've never seen him like this," Hayley said, shaking her head.

"You just have to know how to handle them," Marla said. "Now, your cat seems perfectly healthy to me. What seems to be the problem?"

"He's having bladder issues," Hayley said.

"I see, well, that might be something more psychological," Marla said, an accusing look in her eye. "Is everything okay at home?"

Hayley didn't like the idea of a girl who wasn't even interested in going to vet school insinuating it was somehow Hayley's fault that Blueberry was peeing all over her house.

But Hayley held her tongue.

"Everything's fine at home."

Why mention her depressed daughter, her rattled Shih Tzu, and her double workload at the office? No way was she going to give this girl any ammunition to use against her.

"Okay, then. The doctor will see you and Blueberry tomorrow morning. He will be in at seven."

"In the morning?"

"Yes. He's a morning person. And a very hard worker. Just be sure to give us twenty-four hours' notice if you need to cancel. Otherwise, we charge you half the normal fee for a consultation."

"But it's already close to six-thirty. The appointment is in twelve and a half hours."

"I guess you should really try to be here on time, then," Marla said with a sweet, insincere smile.

Hayley returned an equally sweet and insincere smile and lifted the carrier.

As she turned to leave, Blueberry hissed and took a swipe at her through the cage with his claws.

Hayley glanced back at Marla, who raised one eyebrow, her face full of judgment.

Chapter 19

Hayley kept her promise to meet Sabrina at Drinks Like A Fish that evening. She was well aware that the tension between them would be palpable, given the fact she had forced Sal to post her story online that afternoon, and Sabrina would no doubt have seen it. And even if she hadn't, someone would have read it and called or e-mailed her.

Sure enough.

When Hayley walked through the door, she spotted Sabrina sitting atop a bar stool, nursing a gin and tonic, furiously shaking her straw up and down in the ice, grimacing.

No one was tending bar.

Hayley assumed Randy and his bartender, Michelle, were hiding in the back office to avoid Sabrina's wrath.

Hayley bravely marched forward, steeling herself for the inevitable confrontation.

When out of the corner of her eye Sabrina caught sight of Hayley approaching, she whipped around on the stool to face her.

"What a pretty blouse," Hayley said, hoping a simple, innocent compliment might defuse the tension.

No such luck.

"Are you trying to ruin me, Hayley? Is that it? Are you still jealous of me, like you were in high school?"

Hayley couldn't remember ever being jealous of Sabrina, but there was no sense in arguing with her.

"Is this about the column I wrote regarding Bessie Winthrop's death?"

"No, Hayley, this is about you borrowing my Backstreet Boys CD and not returning it! Of course this is about the damn column you wrote! You have compromised my professional reputation!"

"I think that may be an overstatement, don't you think, Sabrina?"

"You basically called me incompetent for not conducting an autopsy on Bessie Winthrop!"

"I did no such thing. I merely suggested that in order for her friends and family to get absolute closure, an autopsy might not be a bad idea."

"What friends and family? Everybody hated her!"

"Not me. I liked Bessie," Hayley said, feeling someone needed to stand up for Bessie.

Sabrina jumped off the bar stool and got right up into Hayley's face. She was almost a foot taller, but Hayley wasn't worried. She had always been a scrappy fighter. She knew she could take her if it came to that.

"Well, for your information, Hayley, I spent my entire afternoon having Bessie's body transferred back to me from the funeral home and spending county funds my department doesn't have conducting a preliminary autopsy on her."

Hayley was thrilled. Her column did the trick. It forced Sabrina to get off her butt and take Bessie's death seriously.

"And?"

"And you were right. Somebody did kill Bessie."

Hayley gasped.

She was right.

Finally.

Sabrina was confirming her suspicions.

"I knew it!"

"And I know who did it," Sabrina said, taking a step back from Hayley, grabbing her drink off the bar and downing it.

"Who?"

"Bessie. Bessie killed herself, but it wasn't a suicide. No, Bessie's own bad choices killed her. She didn't take care of herself. She didn't exercise. She ate way too many fats and sugar and processed foods."

Hayley frowned.

"She had a heart attack, Hayley. I knew it from the moment I opened her up. You should have seen how clogged her arteries were. It was disgusting."

"But Bessie wrote me a note. She was afraid someone was trying to kill her."

"Maybe that's true, but he or she didn't have the chance to get the job done before Bessie's body gave out. I'm sorry to disappoint you, Hayley, but there is absolutely no foul play involved here."

"I'm sorry I doubted you, Sabrina," Hayley said, waving at Randy, who poked his head out the swinging kitchen doors to see if Sabrina was still in the bar.

"I used to think it was cute that you fancied yourself some kind of amateur sleuth, investigating local murders, but let me tell you something. It stopped being cute the minute your shenanigans put my reputation as a county official on the line. From here on in, please leave the crime scenes to the professionals. Are we clear?"

Hayley nodded.

"Really, Hayley, I know you looked up to me and all my accomplishments in high school. Cheerleader, drama club, student council vice president, fluent in five different languages, and third runner-up in the Miss Maine Teen USA Pageant. And I am acutely aware that some of that acclaim may have rubbed you the wrong way. I saw that resentful look in your eye as you watched me being crowned prom queen in that Christian

Dior dress my gay uncle sent to me from New York as my graduation present. But seriously, honey, it's time to let go."

And with that, Sabrina grabbed Hayley by the arm, pulled her close, and planted a kiss on her cheek. "Call me when you've gotten over all this and we can try to be friends again. I still think the world of you."

Sabrina spun around and sashayed out the door.

There was a lot Hayley wanted to tell her. Like she wasn't even in the school gym when Sabrina was crowned prom queen. She was outside on the athletic field doing tequila shots with Mona and Liddy and their dates.

But why stain Sabrina's obviously happy, totally skewed memories of how Hayley lived in her shadow?

Hayley was more interested in proving Sabrina wrong. It would be an uphill battle. An autopsy was certainly conclusive evidence. However, a voice inside Hayley kept screaming at her that there was more to Bessie's death than heart disease.

And now she was more determined than ever to get to the bottom of it.

Island Food & Spirits
by
Hayley Powell

Last night I was rifling through my old recipe file and I came across one that made me smile. Or at least it does now. Last summer . . . not so much.

It was right during the middle of tourist season on the island, and I read in the paper that one of my all-time favorite chefs from the Food Network was actually coming to Bar Harbor to hold a one-day cooking class. Well, needless to say, I immediately registered online for the class. There was no way I was going to miss an opportunity to meet my favorite kitchen master up close and personal.

Chef Carlos Ferucci was a guest chef on TV all the time and his handsome Italian good looks and sizzling sex appeal made him a favorite among women from all over the world. Many times I fell asleep on the couch while watching one of his shows, dreaming of the two of us cooking up a storm together . . . among other things.

Chef Carlos also owned a five-star restaurant in Portland, Maine, named L'aragosta (which sounds so sexy when he says it, but it really only means "lobster" in Italian). Everyone on the island who made the trip to Portland always tried to secure reservations and dine in his posh restaurant, which had become famous for the surprise twists in his Italian dishes.

There was no menu when dining at L'aragosta. You were served whatever original dish Chef Carlos created specially for that evening, which just added to the excitement. Well, that and watching him glide around the restaurant making sure all the diners were enjoying their mouthwatering meals.

The girls and I were lucky enough to get a table one night about a year ago during a shopping trip to Portland. I must admit when I saw him in person, I was a goner. He was even more handsome in person than on television!

When the day of the class finally arrived, I was the first to show up at the local Bar Harbor restaurant hosting his class. Eventually the other five women who also signed up arrived. I didn't know any of them. They were all summer residents, and much older than me. When Chef Carlos breezed through the door and said in his deep, sexy, Italian-accented voice, *"Buongiorno,"* I batted my eyes like a schoolgirl with a big crush. That was the moment I became determined to get this big hunk of beef to notice me with my cool attitude and mad cooking skills.

Chef Carlos got right down

to business and requested that we all choose four ingredients that we felt did not go together and bring them back to our respective stations. I very carefully chose anchovies, bread crumbs, dried chili peppers, and chocolate.

Chef Carlos then surprised us. He ordered everyone to prepare a dish for him in sixty minutes. We were allowed to use other ingredients from the kitchen, but the four items we chose were mandatory for our dish. My eyes bugged out of my head! This was just like that Food Network show *Chopped,* and I definitely had not signed up for that at all! I never saw this coming! I glanced over at the other women, who had sly smiles on their faces. All of them suspected what the chef was up to, so they managed to pick predictable items such as canned tomato sauce, onions, green peppers, chicken. Everything to prepare the perfect pasta meal!

Chef Carlos yelled, "Go!" The other ladies scrambled off, giggling and laughing, to fetch whatever else would complement their dish. I just stared miserably at my chosen ingredients. This was going to be a disaster! I had no chance of winning!

I wish I could tell you I was the underdog who came up from behind to win the contest with my unique pasta creation! Sadly, however, it was not meant to be. When Chef Carlos got to my chocolate pasta with anchovies dish, he carefully took a bite, chewed, and looked deep into my eyes. I wanted to melt, but not in a good way. I wanted to melt and disappear into the floor. He then placed his fork down and, without a word, moved on to the next person, ultimately declaring Muffy's chicken artichoke pasta the winner.

Well, a few months later while I was preparing dinner, I was half listening to the television, which, of course, was tuned to the Food Network. As I was getting ready to place the meat loaf on the counter to cool, I heard a familiar, sexy, Italian-accented voice say, "This week I want to prepare

'Chef Carlos's Chocolate Pasta with Anchovies,' which is the number one best-selling dish in my restaurant." I let out a scream so loud that poor Leroy jumped down from the couch and raced out of the room. I dropped the meat loaf on the floor and ran to stand in front of the television, staring in disbelief as I watched Chef Carlos add all of the ingredients I had used that day to make my own chocolate pasta dish.

Now, I understand if you don't believe me, but I swear it's true. I guess I should just be flattered that a famous chef thought my culinary disaster was such a tasty dish that it is now the most popular item on the menu in his world-famous restaurant.

If ever there was a time for something to calm the nerves, this was it. I retrieved my new bottle of Marenco Pineto Brachetto d'Acqui, a sweet, sparkling red wine from Piedmont, which I had picked up at House Wine on Main Street on my way home that evening. I popped the cork and poured myself a glass. Raising it high into the air, I said, "*Salute*, Chef Ferucci! Until we meet again!"

Chef Carlos's Chocolate Pasta with Anchovies

<u>Ingredients</u>

1 pound penne pasta (or your favorite pasta)
3 tablespoons extra-virgin olive oil
2 cloves garlic, chopped
2 dried chili peppers, chopped
8 anchovies, minced
2 cups good dark chocolate (at least 70%), chopped
½ cup fine bread crumbs
Fresh parsley, chopped for garnish

In a large pot of salted boiling water, cook your penne. While pasta is cooking, in another saucepan, heat the olive oil on medium. Reduce to medium-low heat and add your garlic, being careful not to burn it. Sauté your garlic, add the chili peppers and anchovies. Cook until the garlic is golden and anchovies have almost dissolved. Add your chocolate. Stir until melted, then add the bread crumbs.

Just before your pasta is al dente, drain and add to the saucepan. Stir it all together, until mixed very well. Serve, topping with the fresh parsley.

As they say in Italy, *"Mangia!"*

Chapter 20

The following morning when Hayley drove Blueberry back over to the vet's office for his appointment, Dr. Palmer still wasn't in. Marla instructed Hayley to fill out the necessary paperwork and told her she could pick up Blueberry on her lunch hour. If the doctor prescribed medication and it wasn't ready, Hayley could always stop by after work.

Hayley felt she was leaving Blueberry in good hands.

Especially since he was licking Marla's fingers.

What on earth did he like about her so much?

Hayley then raced home, yelled at the kids to get up and get dressed, and then jumped into the bathtub for a fast shower before heading off to work. The water was cold and she shivered as she lathered up with bodywash. She prayed there wasn't something wrong with the water heater. After rinsing off, she shut off the water and stepped out of the tub, grabbing a plush white towel off the rack to dry herself.

She suddenly heard loud guffaws coming from downstairs.

She ran the towel over her wet, matted hair, shook it out, and then pulled on her robe. She tied it around her waist and opened the bathroom door. She popped her head out.

Hayley heard Dustin gasping for air as if he was unable to breathe.

"Is everything all right down there?"

Dustin was still gasping.

"Dustin?"

"Everything's fine," Gemma shouted before erupting into a fit of giggles.

Hayley couldn't believe it.

Gemma was laughing at something.

Finally a crack in the armor.

Some humor to bring her back to a semblance of normalcy.

Perhaps whatever was bothering her had finally been resolved.

Her kids were actually bonding over something ridiculously funny, and she was grateful for that.

Hayley slid on her fuzzy slippers and shuffled down the stairs to see what TV show she had to thank for snapping her daughter out of her doldrums.

The television in the living room was shut off

when Hayley hit the landing. She veered toward the kitchen, where the kids were seated at the table, staring at Dustin's iPad.

Dustin tried taking a sip of juice, but then his eye caught something on the screen. He spit it out, dribbling juice all down the front of his t-shirt.

Hayley couldn't help but laugh herself. She rarely saw her kids so hysterical.

She turned the iPad toward her to get a look at what was entertaining them so much.

Her face froze.

It was a YouTube video.

The ill-fated taping of Bessie Winthrop's chocolate-baking segment.

And at two minutes and thirty-five seconds into the video, Hayley was throwing up brown goop all over the place and wreaking havoc on the set.

"Oh, dear God, no!" Hayley cried.

"You're a YouTube sensation, Mom! Already forty thousand hits!" Dustin said, eyes wide, totally impressed. "That's awesome!"

"Forty thousand?" Hayley said, her heart sinking.

Dustin tapped a key. "I just refreshed the page. Now you're up to sixty-two thousand!"

Hayley slammed her fist down on the kitchen table. "Those little punks! They promised to erase this take."

"Mom, you can't blame them. This is pure gold! It's all about racking up hits on their channel.

They couldn't keep something this great under wraps!"

Now that Hayley was in the room, Gemma was making a concerted effort not to smile or laugh anymore. However, as her eyes drifted back toward the iPad screen, she couldn't help herself. She couldn't hold it in. She buried her face in her hands and let loose, howling.

"This isn't happening. Do you think a lot of local people have seen this?"

"People all over the world are seeing this! You're famous now!"

Hayley used to dream of being famous.

For her cooking.

Not for eating too much chocolate and throwing up on camera.

Be careful what you wish for.

Hayley tried not looking at the iPad screen anymore. Why punish herself? But it was like a six-car pileup. As traumatic as it was to stare at the carnage, she just couldn't help herself.

At that moment in the video, the on-screen Hayley foolishly thought she was done being sick and began apologizing to Bessie; but then she instantly threw her hand to her mouth and began spasming all over again. She was struggling to keep the chocolate down with unsuccessful results.

Dustin fell off his chair, hitting the floor, holding his sides as he laughed uproariously. "This is classic. I already posted it on Facebook. All my friends are sharing it."

"I'm so happy you kids find such enjoyment in your mother's humiliation. I'll be sure to remember this."

Gemma got up from the table and grabbed her backpack. "I'm going to be late for the bus."

"You want me to give you a ride to school today?" Hayley asked, looking for any excuse to stop watching the YouTube video.

"No, thanks," Gemma said, her back to her mother. She was out the door in a flash.

Well, at least Gemma laughed a little this morning. Granted, it was at Hayley's expense, but she was happy she was at least able to get a smile out of her sullen daughter.

Hayley slapped the protective cover over the iPad and handed it to Dustin. "That's enough of that. Shouldn't you be more in a rush? The bus will be here any minute."

"Can you give me a ride to school?"

"No, I want to take Leroy for a walk before work."

"But you were going to give Gemma a ride!"

"Yes. But she didn't post that video on Facebook. Now move. Do not miss the bus!"

Dustin sighed and then slung his Avengers backpack over his shoulder and dragged his feet out the door.

"Have a good day," Hayley chirped.

"I'm already having one," Dustin said, smiling. "I have a famous mom!"

"Don't forget your lunch," Hayley said, picking up a brown paper bag and tossing it to Dustin, who caught it with one hand and shot out the door.

Hayley padded to the laundry room, fished some sweatpants and a t-shirt out of the dryer, and dropped her robe. She got dressed and then slid into some winter boots and a heavy coat before yanking on a thick brown wool hat over her still-damp hair. Then she crossed to the coat-rack in the foyer and picked up Leroy's long, metal-studded blue leash. Leroy was already at the front door, with his tiny tail wagging and his tongue panting with excitement.

He was probably just happy Blueberry was MIA this morning.

Hayley hooked the leash around Leroy's collar.

It was already seven-thirty. She had to be at work by eight, so it was going to be a short walk. The temperature had dropped overnight. There was frost on all the windows of the houses in the neighborhood. Leroy didn't seem to mind the cold. He trotted along, just happy to be out.

Hayley tried to put the YouTube video out of her mind. The whole thing would probably blow over quickly and her life would hopefully get back to normal.

A car approached and two kids were in the

backseat as their mother drove. At the sight of Hayley, the kids started pointing excitedly at her as if she were SpongeBob SquarePants or some other celebrity. Hayley turned around after the car passed her. She saw the kids, with their chubby, openmouthed faces now pressed up against the back window, laughing hysterically and still pointing at her.

Perhaps it would take a little more time than she originally thought for this thing to blow over.

Hayley cut through a side street and into a stretch of woods, heading for a thicket of trees, where Leroy could do his business.

She suddenly sensed a presence.

Someone behind her.

Following her.

She looked back.

There was no one in sight.

Seriously?

The YouTube video had been posted online less than twelve hours ago and she already had a stalker?

She heard someone cough.

Hayley spun her head around in the direction of the sound, but she still saw no one. Leroy lifted his leg and let out a steady stream of urine, soaking the exposed root of a pine tree. The dog had a happy, relieved look on his face.

Hayley's eyes focused on a puff of white smoke coming from behind a tree, just to her right.

Was someone hiding behind it smoking a cigarette?

Then she realized it wasn't smoke at all.

It was water vapor from someone breathing out the cold air.

Hayley gulped.

Someone *was* following her and trying to stay out of sight.

"Who's there?" Hayley shouted, tightening Leroy's leash.

Under normal circumstances, at the sound of his master being threatened, Leroy would start barking incessantly, protecting Hayley, scaring off anyone who might want to do her harm.

But that was before Blueberry.

Whatever sense of bravery Leroy once possessed was long gone; it had been completely knocked out of him by a feline terrorist. He was scared of everything now. As he finished tinkling the last few drops, he dashed behind Hayley's leg and remained there in case there was imminent danger.

Hayley went for her cell phone in her coat pocket, but then she remembered she didn't bring it with her.

But the stalker didn't know that.

"I'm calling 911 right now," Hayley warned,

pretending to be punching numbers into her phone.

"No need for that," a man's voice said before Cody Donovan stepped out from behind the tree.

"Cody, you scared me silly," Hayley said, breathing a sigh of relief. "What the hell are you doing out here? You live clear across town."

Cody stepped forward. He looked somewhat disheveled. He had bed head; there were sleepy seeds caked to his face; underneath his half-open gray winter coat, he was wearing pajamas, which had little cartoon deer all over them.

"I set my alarm extra early this morning and slipped out before my wife realized where I was going."

"So, where are you going?"

"Here. To see you."

"Me? Why?"

Cody raced forward, grabbing Hayley's hands in his and squeezing them so tightly that her bones nearly cracked.

"I need to talk to you. About us."

"Cody, unless you want to approve me for a mortgage refinance, we have nothing to talk about."

Cody wasn't going to let it go that easily. "I never stopped having feelings for you, Hayley. You must know that."

"Actually, no, I didn't. You're married. . . ."

Cody let go of her hands and threw his arms around her in a bear hug, drawing her close enough so that he could plant a wet, sloppy kiss on her lips.

Hayley's arms were pinned so she couldn't punch him.

The next best thing was a swift kick to the shins.

Cody howled in pain, releasing her.

"I'm going to forget this ever happened, Cody. I suggest you do too."

"But what if I can't? Do you know how long it took for me to get the nerve up to do this?!"

"Well, find a way!"

"I love you, Hayley."

Oh, man. Can this day get any worse?

"If you ever follow me or try to kiss me again, I swear I'm going to call your wife, Kerry, and let her know you won't leave me alone. And you know her family has lots of powerful legal connections and can make sure she gets everything in the divorce settlement—and I mean *everything,* including that ninety-two-foot twin-masted schooner her Dad gave you, which you're so proud of! No, forget *settlement.* She'll get *everything,* and all you'll be left with are those tacky deer pajamas you're wearing!"

This stopped Cody.

He nodded, eyes downcast, like a scolded boy; he then turned on his heels and scampered away through the woods.

Hayley prayed that would be the end of that.

But she knew she was just fooling herself.

Chapter 21

Hayley spent the entire day writing her own column as well as Bruce's while dodging phone calls and e-mails about her embarrassing performance on YouTube. To appease Sal, she chose to focus on the police department's progress on the recent pharmacy theft. Her only break was picking up Blueberry on her lunch hour and taking him home. That left little time for her to consider the clues she found at Bessie Winthrop's house.

By the following morning, she had a slight break in her workload. She was finally able to spend a few minutes going over her plan of attack. The lawsuit Bessie was embroiled in with her neighbors Mark and Mary Garber was first and foremost in her mind.

Hayley knew the Garbers socially. She was often invited to their deck chat, a nightly cocktail hour on the open-air deck built on the side of their house, where friends would gather to discuss and dissect the latest and juiciest gossip in town. She hadn't attended in a while; and even though they didn't let the nippy winter weather stop them, she had heard through the grapevine they had recently put a hold on their late-afternoon soirees after one of their guests came down with pneumonia and had to be hospitalized. Even though there was no way for them to be legally responsible, they were probably a little skittish, since they were already knee-deep in one lawsuit and probably paying a healthy chunk of their life savings to a lawyer.

Hayley had to find another way besides deck chat to finagle an invitation to the Garbers' house in order to poke around.

She pulled up her list of contacts on her computer and scrolled down for the Garbers' home number. Sal was out of the office for a shareholders' meeting, so it was safe to make a personal call. She punched in the number and waited. After six rings she was about to hang up, since there didn't appear to be any voice mail set up. However, there was a *click* eventually and she heard a raspy voice slur, "I told you, I am on the National Do Not Call Registry, so I couldn't care less about your stupid product. If you call here again, I will have you arrested for violating my rights. Do you hear me?"

"Mary? It's Hayley Powell."

"Who?"

"Hayley Powell."

"Oh, Hayley, I'm sorry! I just keep getting calls from these annoying telemarketers and it's pissing me off. I told Mark to make them stop, and he said he put our number on the Do Not Call Registry, so they shouldn't be bugging us anymore. Oh, wait, maybe I meant to tell him and forgot. Sometimes after a couple of bottles of wine, I imagine conversations. Is this really you, Hayley?"

"Yes. You're not imagining it."

"Good. Because I've already had two bottles of wine." Mary snickered.

It wasn't even noon.

"I haven't spoken to you in a while and I thought I'd check in and see how you're doing?"

"Well, as you know, we've canceled deck chat until Memorial Day because of what happened to Becky Simpson. What a wimp. I mean, I'm sorry she got sick and everything, but did she have to blame us for making her sit outside in January? We were kind enough to invite her, but she really didn't have to come if she was afraid of being out in the cold. Jeez. Well, you know her. Always making trouble. And what is it with her and grape-flavored vodka? Who drinks that stuff? We always had to stock up on it whenever she was coming over. Talk about pricey! We're not the Rockefellers! I'm sorry. Who am I talking to again?"

"Hayley Powell."

"Right. Sorry. I heard you found that pain-in-the-ass Bessie Winthrop's dead body. Another troublemaker. Good riddance."

"Yes. The scuttlebutt around town is that you and Mark were involved in some kind of a lawsuit with Bessie."

"Yeah, she was all over us because we wanted to add one lousy addition to our house and it was going to block her view. We've been working our butts off renovating this money trap! And just when we saved enough money to add on a third floor, Bessie files a lawsuit and puts the brakes on everything."

"That must have infuriated you."

"I wanted to kill that nasty bitch."

There was a long dramatic pause as Hayley let Mary's last words sink in for a moment.

"You hated her that much?"

Mary seemed to catch herself, even in her drunken state. "Well, I mean, I barely knew her." Then she was off and running again. "But she was making our lives miserable. Not only was she suing us, but her place was basically a junkyard and stunk to high heaven with all those cats roaming around. Everyone's property values on the street were plummeting because of her."

"Well, now that she's dead and gone, I guess you can proceed with your addition," Hayley said.

"Hallelujah!" Mary sang, taking a beat to apparently pour herself another glass of wine.

Hayley racked her brain trying to come up with a way to get herself invited to Mary's house so she could search the place and see if she could possibly come up with any evidence besides the lawsuit that might connect them to Bessie's death.

"Well, I hope to see you and Mark soon."

"How about Saturday?"

"You mean tomorrow?"

"Mark and I are having a few people over for dinner before the Hayseed Ball. You should come and bring that handsome caretaker guy you've been shacking up with."

"Lex moved to Vermont. We're not seeing each other anymore. And we never lived together."

"Right. I forgot. So bring that new guy, the one from Bucksport, Liddy's cousin."

"I'm definitely *not* seeing him."

"What are you talking about? I ran into Liddy at the hairdresser's last week and she told me you two were practically engaged."

"Yes, but, unfortunately, that was before I met him."

"Well, come stag then. I don't care. You can borrow Mark if you want. I'd love to be single for one night and see what kind of hot manly stud I can rustle up at the ball."

The annual Hayseed Ball in Bar Harbor was one of the most attended social events of the season. Guests got all dolled up in period costumes—like plug-hatted farmers in peg-top trousers, while their female partners twirled in crinoline and gingham. Everyone engaged in old-fashioned dances, including quadrilles, two-steps, and contras.

"Thanks, Mary, I would love to come, as long as you don't mind having an uneven number for dinner."

"Like I could give a crap? I always make too much food, but bring a bottle of wine. I never seem to have enough. I really don't know why."

"Will do," Hayley said, hanging up. She was not looking forward to sticking out as the only single person at the Garbers' dinner party. And she had absolutely no intention of attending the ball afterward, where it would be glaringly obvious she was a wallflower.

But for right now, it was the only avenue she had to get inside the Garbers' house and investigate. She had to accept their invitation because the Garbers had such a clear motive for wanting to see Bessie pushing up daisies.

Mary wasn't hiding her hatred of Bessie. But that was because the police and the coroner had closed the case and so emphatically ruled out homicide as a cause of death.

Maybe Mary Garber was convinced she was in the clear and had just beaten a murder rap.

It was up to Hayley to prove Mary wrong.

Chapter 22

Sal called and told Hayley he was not coming back to the office after his meeting with the shareholders, so that left all afternoon for Hayley to put both columns to bed and leave work a little early. She received a call from Dr. Palmer's assistant Marla informing her that Blueberry's prescription finally was ready. She swung by the vet's office to pick it up on her way home.

When she walked through the door, she spotted Marla sitting behind her desk in some new scrubs. These featured Snoopy and various Peanuts characters.

Hayley considered introducing Marla to Cody Donovan. At least the two had something in common. They both favored silly cartoon images on their clothing.

Hayley spied a white bag stapled closed sitting on the edge of Marla's desk.

When Marla spotted Hayley entering through

the door, she quickly seized the bag and threw it at Hayley. "Here you go. Have a nice weekend!"

Marla was certainly in a hurry to get rid of her, so Hayley nodded, thanked her, and turned to leave.

"Hayley?"

Hayley turned to see Dr. Palmer coming out of his office.

Marla was scowling.

No wonder she wanted to get Hayley out of the office as fast as she could. The good doctor was around and she was hoping to avoid them running into each other.

This was one jealous assistant.

"Hello, Dr. Palmer," Hayley said.

"Aaron, please," he said, smiling.

My God, he has such perfectly straight, blindingly white teeth.

"*Mrs.* Powell just dropped by for Blueberry's medicine. Everything seems to be in order, so there's nothing else she needs. Nice seeing you again, Mrs. Powell. Say hello to Blueberry and Leroy for us."

"Okay, thanks," Hayley said awkwardly before turning to go again.

"Hayley, wait . . . ," Dr. Palmer—no, Aaron—said.

Hayley turned back around, but all she could focus on was Marla's fuming face, turning red with anger, her white knuckles gripping the edge of her desk. She was frustrated that she was so close to having Hayley out the door with no fanfare and now her plans were completely thwarted.

"I . . . I w-was wondering . . . I'm kind of new in t-town . . . ," Aaron said, stammering.

Like he was nervous.

It was *so* cute.

He was *so* cute.

"The Hayseed Ball is tomorrow night, and I thought maybe if you weren't busy or weren't already going with someone else . . ."

He was asking her on a date.

Hayley couldn't believe it.

Neither could Marla, who gasped so loud that it distracted Aaron and he turned and looked at her.

"Is everything all right, Marla?"

"Yes, fine. I'm just going to take a quick bathroom break."

Marla stood up and slowly walked away from her desk, glancing back once and shaking her head as if pleading, *demanding*, Hayley not trespass on what she clearly considered her territory.

"Anyway," Aaron said. "If you'd like to go—"

"I already have plans," Hayley said, the words falling out of her mouth.

Wait.

She couldn't leave it like that.

That sounded like she was turning him down.

"I mean, some friends of mine, the Garbers,

are having me over for dinner before the ball. They said I could bring a . . . friend if I wanted, so I'm sure you'd be welcome. . . ."

"And then you would accompany me to the ball after dinner?"

"Uh, sure, yes, that would be lovely."

Lovely. *Did I really just say "lovely"?*

She might as well be wearing a hoopskirt and white gloves and bow to him at this point as if he were Mr. Darcy and she were Elizabeth Bennet.

"Excellent. I'm sure Marla has your address in Leroy and Blueberry's files. When is dinner?"

"Seven."

"Great. I'll pick you up at six forty-five. I'm really looking forward to it, Hayley."

"Me too," Hayley said, trying not to bubble over with too much euphoria and say something silly or stupid like she was usually prone to do.

She felt her mouth opening.

No, don't.

Just keep your lips shut tight and don't blow this incredible moment by talking.

Marla careened back around the corner at that moment, saving Hayley from herself.

"Do you have Hayley's home address, Marla? We're going out tomorrow night."

"Oh yes, I . . . Yes, I do. I'll make sure to text it to your phone so you have it," Marla said.

Marla looked like she was going to throw up.

It was a good thing Hayley didn't think to

record Marla heaving her lunch on her iPhone camera. She just might be tempted to post it on YouTube in order to take the heat off herself.

Suddenly the YouTube humiliation didn't seem so important.

She had a date with a handsome, sexy doctor.

Things were definitely looking up.

184   DEATH OF A CHOCOHOLIC

Chapter 23

Hayley felt incredibly foolish combing through Mark and Mary Garber's medicine cabinet while dressed in a vintage rockabilly blue-and-white floral huge sweep-circle swing dress, with a frilly white apron tied around it, and matching blue clogging shoes. And then there was the woven-straw Minnie Pearl hat, complete with the price tag dangling off it. She didn't have much of a choice. This was the night of one of Bar Harbor's most popular winter events, the Hayseed Ball. So there was no point in showing up in a simple black cocktail dress.

Hayley didn't find much in the bathroom, so she tried to move quietly to the bedroom, but it was impossible to be quiet in clogging shoes. Luckily, downstairs the Garbers were on their third round of drinks, so the volume of the chatter and laughter was reaching earsplitting levels, which drowned out Hayley banging around upstairs searching for clues.

Her date for the evening, Dr. Aaron Palmer, was probably wondering what was taking her so damn long just to powder her nose, but this was Hayley's one and only chance to see if she could drum up some kind of tangible evidence besides the lawsuit linking the Garbers to the murder.

If, in fact, it was a murder.

She still had no concrete proof, and all the current evidence went against her theory of foul play. But Hayley had a strong feeling, a persistent intuition, and she was determined to prove herself right.

She wished she could just forget it. Accept the facts as they appeared. It would be a lot easier. She could just enjoy her first of what she hoped would be many more dates with the handsome, new vet.

When he showed up at her door, the vet was wearing a brown-and-green long-sleeved flannel shirt, jean overalls, and black boots. He was chewing comically on a hayseed. In Hayley's eyes he might as well have been wearing a stylish black Carlyle tuxedo.

He even playfully used a country drawl as he remarked how "dang pretty" Hayley looked in her smock as he took her by the hand and led her to a weathered, old pickup truck with bales of hay stacked in the flatbed.

Man, he went all out preparing for this ball.

And it did the trick.

Hayley hadn't experienced a hot farmer/hick fantasy since she drooled over Tom Wopat, one of the beer-guzzling, fast-riding, sweet-talking brothers on that old *Dukes of Hazzard* show, which she caught in reruns when she was in high school.

Aaron opened the squeaky passenger-side door of the truck and held it open for Hayley, who curtsied before climbing in and straightening out her dress. The hoop kept rising up; so to keep from revealing her white silk panties to Aaron, she had to force it down with her hands as she sat there.

He hopped into the driver's seat and tried three times to start the truck before the engine finally sputtered to life.

The Hayseed Ball was established in 1894 and hosted by forty Hayseeders, most descendants of the local men who started it. The only way to get an invitation was to be a guest of one of the Hayseeders. The origin of the event began as a way for locals to blow off steam in midwinter after all the wealthy colony people, like the Rockefellers and the Fords, had locked up their summer estates after the season and were long gone. A lot of locals were resentful of being treated like "hayseeds" by the rich folks, so the ball was a creative way for them to thumb their noses at the well-to-do when they weren't around. The attendees mocked the rich folks' impression of the locals, who fished and gardened and generally looked after the upper-class residents' every need.

Mark and Mary Garber were new to town and had no familial connections to the Hayseeders. However, Mark was so gregarious and likeable, one elderly Hayseeder, who had no children or brothers to pass his membership onto, willed his to Mark after Mark painted his house the previous fall for no money. So now Mark was a bona fide Hayseeder, and this was his first ball. A celebratory dinner beforehand for his personal guests to the ball was a must.

"Hayley, what the hell are you doing?" Mary Garber slurred, sloshing a glass of bourbon around, her hand on her hip. She was wearing a red blouse with puffy sleeves and a skirt with two mini-tiered ruffles, trimmed with ricrac in navy, green, and red and layered with white eyelets. She couldn't have looked more adorable.

Or accusatory as she stared at Hayley rifling through the dresser drawer in her bedroom.

"I . . . I was looking f-for . . . ," Hayley stammered.

She was caught red-handed.

It would be fruitless to lie at this point.

It was better just to confess and take her licks.

"I knew you were having a lot of problems with Bessie Winthrop, and I'm still not entirely convinced she died of natural causes, and so I thought since I was here, I could take the opportunity to look around and see if—"

"You think Mark and I bumped her off?" Mary's eyes widened.

Hayley shook her head emphatically. "No, not at all, it's just that—"

"You do! You think we killed her because she was suing us!"

Hayley's mouth was open, but no words were coming out.

She wanted to say something, but she didn't know what.

"That is so . . . exciting!" Mary squealed, swigging the rest of her bourbon and then grabbing Hayley by the hand and dragging her back down the stairs. "Everyone, you have to hear this! It's hilarious!"

"Mary, please, I don't think we should tell people. . . ."

But it was too late.

Mary had a viselike grip on Hayley's wrist as she pulled her into the dining room, where her other guests, including local lawyer Ted Rivers, a Hayseeder himself, his wife, Sissy, along with Aaron, Mary's husband, Mark, and another couple Hayley had just met, were seated at the long table.

"Mark, you're going to love this!" Mary said, still grasping Hayley. "We all know Hayley is Bar Harbor's very own Jessica Fletcher, amateur sleuth at large, investigating murders and keeping the bad guys off the street. . . ."

Mark nodded, smiling.

Aaron watched, curious about where this was going.

"Well, it seems that Hayley thinks we did it! You and me! We somehow knocked Bessie off because she was giving us such a hard time about our renovation plans!"

There was a stunned silence.

The guests just sat in their seats, digesting this revelation.

"I caught her going through our drawers, hoping to find some kind of incriminating evidence the cops could use to arrest us! Isn't that the funniest thing you ever heard? How wonderful! Come on, admit it! You've all wanted to be murder suspects in an Agatha Christie novel. Am I right?"

More silence.

And then Mark chuckled.

Which paved the way for the rest of the guests to join in.

Pretty soon everybody was laughing.

Full-on belly laughing.

Hayley was not so naive to think they were laughing with her.

They were definitely laughing at her.

And at the absurdity of her actually believing

the Garbers were a pair of coldhearted killers a la Bonnie and Clyde.

In hindsight it did seem a tad foolish.

The laughter was building, mostly because all the guests were feeling no pain from their cocktails. In fact, Mark's guffawing was so infectious that pretty soon the entire room was filled with an explosion of cackles and giggles and howling.

Only one person wasn't doubled over, roaring with laughter.

Aaron stood up from the table, crossed to Hayley, and whispered in her ear, "Is this the only reason you agreed to come out with me tonight? So you could snoop around the Garbers' house?"

"No, Aaron. I swear. I mean, yes, it did cross my mind that while we were here, I might find a moment to excuse myself and look around. But in all honesty, I was looking forward to spending time with you and getting to know you."

Aaron nodded, but he was frowning.

Not entirely convinced she was telling him the truth.

Chapter 24

Hayley tried her best to put her faux pas at the Garbers' house out of her mind as Aaron escorted her into the Masonic Hall for the Hayseed Ball. The room was decorated with pea brush and enough red, white, and blue balloons for a Republican convention. There was also sand on the dance floor.

Hayley hoped no one would slip and fall and break a hip.

There was a big banner draped across the entrance with the names of the dances, waltzes, and quadrilles, with deliberate spelling mistakes, since Hayseeds were obviously much too stupid and uncultured to be good spellers. A four-piece band played old-school dance music from the Great Depression era. Off to the side was a cash bar and a food table that only offered traditional Hayseeder snacks, such as doughnuts, dried salt codfish, and a cheddar-cheese plate. An old newsreel from the 1930s with clips of breadlines and Shirley Temple was projected on the back white wall of the hall.

Mary made a beeline for Sabrina, who was decked out in a tight-fitting pink lace "Puttin' on the Ritz" flapper dress and a black feathered headband and matching boa. She was on the arm of her husband, who was in a smart gray pin-striped suit, looking nothing like a Hayseeder but rather the reviled enemy. In fact, he looked exactly like the slimy lawyer Richard Gere played in the movie musical *Chicago*. Sabrina must have put the kibosh on dressing like a poor farmer and his wife, despite how out of place they would look.

Hayley watched as Mary chatted with Sabrina.

Sabrina's smile slowly faded.

Hayley knew in her gut what they were talking about.

Especially when Sabrina turned her head in Hayley's direction and did a slow burn, with her eyes boring into her.

"I'll go get us some drinks," Aaron said, crossing to the bar.

Hayley didn't want him to go. Aaron was probably her only protection from the furiously vindictive Sabrina, who was now marching over to her.

"Sabrina, let me explain," Hayley mumbled, defensively putting her hands up in front of her face in case Sabrina tried to take a swing at her.

"You just can't let it go, can you, Hayley? You

are obsessed with your nonstop campaign to smear my good name!"

"This has nothing to do with *you*, Sabrina—"

"This has *everything* to do with me, and you know it!"

The band suddenly started playing "Turkey in the Straw" and a dozen couples lined up and began dancing the Winter Solstice, forming a big square with one couple dancing in the middle.

The music drowned out Sabrina, who at the moment was wagging a finger in front of Hayley's face and rattling off a litany of complaints about Hayley she had harbored since high school.

This did not bode well for their reunion, which was scheduled for next summer.

In a gesture of sympathy, Sabrina's husband, Jerry, finally took Hayley's hand and bowed to her. "May I have this dance, madam?"

Hayley glanced at Sabrina, who stopped yelling at Hayley and spun around to glare at her husband for so rudely interrupting her.

He avoided eye contact, whisking Hayley out onto the dance floor to stomp and whistle and clap with the other couples in the country hoedown.

"That was my attempt to defuse the situation!" Jerry yelled into Hayley's ear over the music.

"I'm betting you pay for that later," Hayley shouted, "dearly!"

"She's just threatened by you, that's all."

"Me? How could she be threatened by me? She's a doctor!"

"Yeah, a doctor who can't cook or write. Those are skills you excel at. The one thing she's good at is finding answers to how or why somebody died. And ever since you started becoming this amateur sleuth—with a pretty good track record, I might add—she feels you're encroaching on her hallowed territory. And it's driving her nuts!"

"I never thought of it that way," Hayley said. "I would never—"

"I know you wouldn't do anything like that intentionally, Hayley. But there is one thing you always need to remember about my wife."

"What's that?"

"She's crazy. I'm not talking about eccentric or weird or quirky. I mean one hundred percent all-out 'someone get a straightjacket' bat-shit crazy! But that doesn't mean I don't love her," Jerry said, laughing.

A man tapped Jerry on the shoulder. "May I cut in?"

It was Cody Donovan.

"No!" Hayley screamed over the music.

But it was too late.

Cody pushed Jerry aside and took Hayley into his arms, sweeping her around the dance floor. She tried to struggle free, but his grip on her was too strong. The more she wiggled, the tighter his arm fastened around her back and he squeezed her hand.

"I didn't mean to scare you the other day, Hayley. I just had to get my feelings for you off my chest."

"Cody, I can't breathe—"

"Just hear me out. I haven't been happy in my marriage for a long, long time. I've forgotten what being happy even feels like. That is, until I see you. And then I'm like one of those animated Valentine's Day e-cards, where the little brown bear is dancing in the meadow and all those little pulsing hearts come flying out of him when he sees the cute-as-pie girl bear in the pink skirt, looking all shy and demure."

"I've never seen an e-card like that, Cody. Now let go."

But he didn't let go.

He was afraid if he did, this would be his last chance to try and win Hayley over, since she was not cooperating with his plan to rekindle a fiery romance.

Suddenly they were in the middle of the square, with all the other dancers stomping their feet and clapping around them. Cody tried to spin Hayley in a circle, but she nailed him in the boot with the heel of her shoe.

He howled in pain, finally letting her go. The band kept playing, but the Hayseeders stopped dancing as Cody hopped around on one foot, moaning.

All eyes were fixed on Hayley.

"I'm sorry. I guess I'm just not a very good dancer," Hayley said to the crowd, shrugging.

"I think it's time we called it a night," Aaron said.

Aaron.

She had forgotten all about him.

He had gone to get them some drinks and then she just left him on his own.

"Aaron, I am so sorry. I didn't mean—"

Then, without warning, like a flash flood, a torrent of red liquid came gushing out of nowhere, splashing Hayley and Aaron. It was sticky and messy and matted her hair and stained her dress. She fished a lemon wedge out of her hairdo, which now looked like a rat's nest.

"Stay away from my husband!" Kerry Donovan bawled as tears streamed down her rosy-red cheeks.

She was holding an empty punch bowl.

Aaron wiped the fruit punch off his face with a handkerchief from the pocket of his overalls and didn't say a word.

Kerry then hurled the punch bowl at Hayley, who ducked sideways. It sailed past her and smashed to pieces on the floor.

The band finally stopped playing to investigate the commotion.

A despondent Kerry Donovan ran out of the Masonic Hall, her high heels clicking.

No one else dared to move.

Aaron finished wiping off his face and then, without saying a word, walked out of the Masonic Hall. Hayley followed him to apologize, but he was in no mood to hear it. He motioned for her to get in the truck and then drove her home.

There was very little conversation on the way.

A halfhearted "Are you warm enough?"

A clearing of the throat.

Within minutes he was dropping her off on her doorstep.

There was a mumbled thank-you and a good-night.

Definitely no kiss on the lips.

Or cheek.

Or anywhere for that matter.

Hayley knew that was pretty much it.

They were done.

So much for the handsome, new vet.

It was good while it lasted.

Chapter 25

The following Monday morning, Hayley got the kids off to school and raced to the bank to withdraw some spending money for lunch. After parking her car in the lot, she fished through her wallet and bag for her ATM card, but she couldn't find it.

She was already running late for work, so she scooted inside the bank, scribbled her information on a withdrawal slip, and lined up behind an elderly woman, who was making a cash deposit and examining every last dollar bill before counting it.

This was going to take all day.

Hayley checked her watch.

It was 8:10 A.M.

Sal was not going to be happy.

Pam Innsbrook, the sweet-natured, helpful bank teller, and a big fan of Hayley's column, removed her NEXT WINDOW PLEASE sign and waved

Hayley over. Hayley sighed with relief as she raced over to Pam and slapped down her withdrawal slip.

"My ATM card has gone AWOL, Pam, so it looks like I have to get some much-needed cash the old-fashioned way."

"Happy to help, Hayley," Pam chirped, picking up the slip of paper and typing numbers into her computer. "By the way, I made your German chocolate cake recipe for my parents at our Sunday family dinner last night, and they just *loved* it!"

"Oh, that's so nice to hear."

"Did you have a good weekend, Hayley?" Pam asked, smiling like the Cheshire cat as she processed the withdrawal and began counting out five ten-dollar bills.

Before Hayley had the chance to answer, Pam slid the small stack of money over to her. Hayley went to pick it up, but Pam kept her finger pressed down on it. "By the way, I heard about what happened at the Hayseed Ball."

"Who told you?"

"Everyone was talking about it on Facebook and Twitter. In fact, Mary Garber was live tweeting from the Masonic Hall at the moment Kerry Donovan doused you and your date with the fruit punch. It just blew up after that. Cody must be so embarrassed. He hasn't left his office all morning. He got here super early and has just been glued to his computer."

Hayley turned around and glanced in the direction of Cody's office. Through the window she saw him rubbing his temples, his eyes closed. He sat there slumped over his desk, looking tired, haggard, and depressed. Hayley imagined he must have spent his entire Sunday being brow-beaten by his shrill, unhinged, paranoid wife.

Cody suddenly opened his eyes and reached for his New England Patriots coffee mug to take a sip and caught Hayley staring.

Hayley whirled back around to face Pam.

"I'd feel sorry for him if I didn't believe his wife had good reason to be suspicious," Pam said, re-tracting her finger so Hayley could pick up her money and stuff it into her wallet.

"So you think he was cheating?" Hayley asked innocently, knowing for a fact he was, based on the pictures that she had found at Bessie's house of him in bed with another woman.

"Well, there are rumors," Pam said, leaning forward and talking out of the side of her mouth.

"You think it may be someone who works here at the bank?"

"Oh no. The tellers see and hear everything. Nothing gets by us. If it was someone at the bank, we'd know it. It has to be someone on the outside. A few weeks ago, Cassie Noveck was answering the phones, when Kerry Donovan called and asked if Cassie would have Cody call her when he got in from his overnight meeting in Portland. The thing is, there was no overnight meeting in Portland. When Cody showed up, he was wearing the same suit as the day before. Except it was wrinkled and his tie was loose and his hair was all mussed up, like he had just gotten out of bed. How stupid does he think we are?"

"I wonder who it could be."

Pam laughed. "Not a clue. Although the girls and I went out for drinks at your brother's bar the other night and made a few guesses. The funniest one was Bessie Winthrop. How ridiculous is that? Can you picture Cody and Bessie together?"

"Why on earth did her name even come up?"

"Well, Tammy Alley, the girl who works as a teller part-time while she's taking a few business courses so she can work her way up to branch manager—well, she saw them having a really nasty fight in the parking lot after the bank closed one evening."

"About what?"

"She couldn't make out what they were arguing about, but she heard Bessie say something about him having sex with another woman and how wrong that was and how hurtful it was. It was as if Cody had cheated on Bessie and they were having a lovers' quarrel. But Tammy couldn't believe that was the case. She thought she must have heard wrong. It had to be about something else. I mean, seriously! Not to speak ill of the dead, but Bessie? With her hideous print caftans and all those cats, not to mention her obsession with chocolate? I just don't buy it."

Hayley wanted to defend her friend. After all, Bessie had dated before. Granted, Wolf Conway wasn't exactly a commendable choice, but they did have a history. Bessie wasn't a nun. Still, Hayley, too, had a hard time believing Bessie and Cody would ever hook up.

Hayley guessed Bessie was probably blackmailing Cody with those photos in order to get him to approve her business loan.

That had to be it.

That's what the fight in the parking lot was about.

But who was the woman?

And did Cody decide to knock off Bessie instead of agreeing to her demands?

Pam's phone rang. She raised a finger for Hayley to hold on for a moment as she picked up the receiver. "Hello, this is Pam."

Pam rolled her eyes, annoyed as someone talked to her on the other end of the line.

Hayley knew exactly who it was.

"Yes, Mr. Donovan," Pam said, shaking her head. "Right away."

She hung up. "He knows we're talking about him, so he's getting nervous. He wants me to bring him a file that he could easily have just looked up on his computer."

"I have to get to work anyway. Thanks, Pam," Hayley said, turning to leave.

Pam put the NEXT WINDOW PLEASE sign back up

and the handful of customers who had lined up while they were talking groaned and sighed before moving to the other two open teller windows.

Hayley was halfway to her car when she felt a sudden presence coming up fast behind her.

Someone grabbed her arm and twisted her around.

It was Cody.

"What were you talking about in there with Pam Innsbrook? I want to know, Hayley. Those hens won't stop gossiping about me and I'm sick of it! What are they saying?"

"I'll tell you what they're *not* talking about. Yet . . . anyway. The fact that Bessie Winthrop was blackmailing you with photos she took of you in a compromising situation with another woman."

Cody's face went white. He looked around to make sure no one heard what Hayley had just said. "You have no idea what you're talking about!"

"I don't?" Hayley said, reaching into her bag and pulling out the photos she had printed at the office from Bessie's digital camera.

Cody's eyes nearly popped out of his head as he snatched the photos from her and stuffed them back deep inside Hayley's bag.

He looked around again, panic-stricken.

"Don't be waving those around, okay?" Cody begged, craning his head around again to see that elderly woman, who was so slow to count her dollar bills to deposit, finally exiting out of the bank and shuffling her way to a Cadillac model from the 1970s. "Can we please go somewhere more private to discuss this?"

"Lead the way," Hayley said.

They walked a few blocks to the town shore path. In the summer the scenic area, with a picture-perfect view of the dark blue Atlantic and the islands dotting the harbor, was packed with strolling tourists, dogs chasing Frisbees, and kids playing on the rocks, looking for snails and tiny fish and seashells. But in the middle of February, on a blustery morning, with the cold winds kicking up, there wasn't a soul around. Most of the houses and mansions set back from the ocean were boarded up and deserted for the winter.

Hayley and Cody stopped and faced each other.

"How did you get your hands on those pictures?" Cody asked, his voice shaking.

"I found them on Bessie's digital camera in her house after she died."

"And do you have the camera in your possession?"

"Why? You looking to destroy the evidence?"

"Hell yes, Hayley! I have a disturbed, spiteful wife who will kill me if she finds concrete proof I've been cheating on her."

"If I send her these photos, at least she'll stop thinking that *I'm* the other woman."

"You wouldn't do that."

"Try me."

"What do you want?"

"The truth. Was Bessie blackmailing you for a business loan?"

Cody nodded. "She must have heard the rumors. I know people at the bank were talking, so she followed me around with a camera until she caught me one night. She must have stood outside the window and just snapped away. What a bitch. The next day she e-mailed me the photos and said if I didn't give her a loan for her silly chocolate business, she'd send those same photos to Kerry."

"Is that when you decided to murder her?"

"*Murder* her? What are you talking about? Bessie died of a heart attack."

"I have reason to believe it may be a homicide."

"What? How?"

"Did you kill her, Cody?"

"No, of course not! I was willing to do anything she wanted to keep my wife from finding out. I had already processed the loan and it was just waiting for her signature, when I heard the news she had died."

"You must have been so relieved," Hayley spat out.

"You better believe it . . . ," Cody said, before catching himself. "I mean, I feel bad and all, but I thought my secret had died with her."

"Who is the woman?"

"What woman?"

"The woman in the photos. Who is it?"

"I can't tell you."

"Did you tell this woman Bessie was blackmailing you? Did she know what was going on?"

"Yes! I was scared. I told her everything. Needless to say, she was very upset and she told me to handle it."

"Well, maybe she didn't trust you to handle it on your own, so *she* decided to take matters into her own hands."

"No! Come on, Hayley! Bessie wasn't murdered. Your own newspaper said so. Just drop it! Please!"

"Her name, Cody. Give me her name!"

"I can't."

"I still have the camera with the pictures on it. I can always turn them over to the police if Bessie's death is reclassified a homicide."

"Hayley, she wouldn't do something like that. Trust me on this. Just leave her out of it."

"Are you two still seeing each other?"

"No! It was a momentary lapse in judgment. We're done. She's very busy. I haven't even seen her lately."

Hayley believed him.

He was a jittery, shaking mess.

And he was too much of a wimp to pull off the perfect murder.

If indeed it was even murder.

Hayley was starting to doubt it herself.

"She's no longer a part of my life. I promise!"

Cody said, reaching out and taking Hayley's hand. "You know I only have eyes for you."

Dear God, not again.

Hayley yanked her hand away.

She was about to slap him in the face, when out of nowhere there was a cracking sound and something whizzed past between them.

"What was that?" Cody asked, looking around.

Another cracking shot.

Another *whoosh* past them.

Like a speeding bullet.

Not *like* a speeding bullet.

It *was* a bullet.

Two bullets.

Someone was shooting at them.

Chapter 26

Hayley and Cody stood frozen in their tracks as another bullet whizzed past them—this one even closer.

Hayley grabbed a fistful of Cody's shirt and pulled them both down to the ground. They covered their heads and frantically looked around in the direction of the shooter. There was a green Dumpster at the edge of the parking lot of Albert Meadow, a picnic area near the edge of the shore path. Hayley saw a head masked in a black ski cap rise up from behind the Dumpster and then a rifle aiming at them.

Another shot.

The bullet tore into the path near Hayley's feet, kicking up dirt and pebbles. One of the tiny rocks flew into Cody's eye and he slapped a hand to his face.

"I've been hit! I've been hit!"

Hayley rolled over to get a look at the wound, but there was no blood.

There was no wound.

"You're fine, Cody! Follow me!"

Hayley crawled on all fours to the edge of the path and jumped over the side, landing hard on the rocks below.

She twisted her ankle on impact, but nothing snapped.

It wasn't broken.

Cody was hanging halfway over the side, foolishly coming face-first, his feet dangling in the air as his hands tried reaching the rocks. Hayley stumbled over and grabbed him in a bear hug, hauling him the rest of the way. He was almost twice her weight, and she thought they would both fall and crack their heads on the sharp, jagged rocks, but Cody landed on his feet. They hugged each other a moment, trying to assess the situation, and how they were going to get out of it.

"What if the shooter chases after us? We're sitting ducks down here!"

"Calm down, Cody! Let me think!".

There was really nowhere for them to go. If the shooter moved to the path and was perched above them, they were cooked. There was also the choice to run for the water and try to swim to safety. But the water was freezing and they would both die of hypothermia before they could reach the first boat or island.

They pressed themselves up against the stone wall of the path.

Waiting.

Listening.

They heard nothing.

Except the calls of a few seagulls.

Waves were slapping hard against the rocks as the tide came in.

And then a car door slammed shut.

An engine roared to life.

Hayley climbed back up the rock face to peer over the edge of the path.

Cody tried stopping her, grabbing her leg. "Hayley, no! Stay out of sight!"

Hayley's head slowly rose up in time to see a car squealing away. She focused on the license number before it veered to the right and back up the road away from Albert Meadow toward Main Street.

She hauled herself back up onto the path. "Shooter's gone, Cody. The coast is clear."

Cody tried following, but his dress shoes kept slipping and sliding on the wet rock face, so Hayley had to grab his hand and hoist him up the rest of the way.

He dusted himself off and straightened his tie. "Did you see who it was?"

"No. But I got the license plate number of the car he was driving. Maine plate. PYT426."

The color drained from Cody's face.

Just like the moment he found out Hayley knew Bessie was blackmailing him.

"What is it, Cody?"

"Nothing. Never mind. I have to get back to work."

Cody tried to walk away, but Hayley stepped in front of him, blocking his escape.

"You know something. Tell me," Hayley said.

"The license number. It's a vanity plate."

"What does it mean?"

"PYT. It means 'Pretty Young Thing,' like the Michael Jackson song. It was my nickname for Kerry. 426. That's her birthday. April twenty-sixth. That was Kerry's car."

"Seriously? That was your *wife* shooting at us?"

"What can I say? I married a jealous woman who is a proud, card-carrying member of the NRA."

Hayley pulled out her phone and called Sergio at the station.

"This is Chief Alvares."

"This is your adoring sister-in-law. I'd like to report a shooting!"

"A shooting? Here? In town? Who got shot?"

"No one. The perp took a few potshots, but nobody got hurt."

Perp.

Hayley loved using police lingo.

It made her feel like Mariska Hargitay, her idol, on that last standing *Law & Order* show.

"I know who it was too. Kerry Donovan."

"Do you know where I can find her?"

Hayley turned to Cody. "What's your address, Cody?"

"45 Bowles Avenue."

"45 Bowles, Sergio. She should be pulling into the driveway any minute."

"Okay, Hayley. I'll head over there myself. Wait. Who was she shooting at?"

"Me."

"Why am I not surprised? I should have heard that coming."

"'Seen,' Sergio. You should have *seen* that coming."

"Seen what?"

"Never mind."

"Anything else you want to tell me?"

Hayley thought about filling him in on Bessie's blackmail scheme, but she knew Cody would freak out if she spoke up now. Best to wait until she had more proof that Bessie was, in fact, murdered.

"Not at the moment. You just go save our town from wrongdoers, you strapping, hunky Brazilian stud."

"I see you've been talking to your brother. He calls me that all the time. Bye. For now."

There was a *click*.

Hayley dropped the phone into her coat pocket.

"Is he going over to my house to arrest her?"

"I'm afraid so, Cody. She tried to kill us."

A smile crept across Cody's face.

"What's that?" Hayley asked.

"What?"

"That smile on your face."

"What smile? I'm not smiling."

"Yes, you are. The sides of your mouth are pointing upward. You look like the Joker!"

"I'm *not* smiling!"

Hayley rummaged through her bag for a compact and flipped it open, pointing the mirror in front of Cody's face. He glanced at his reflection. He tried to frown, but he couldn't. It was like Bell's palsy. No matter how hard he tried to adjust his expression, his face still wouldn't move.

"You can't even fake it. You're happy she's going to jail, aren't you? She's been nothing but a pain in your butt with all her jealousy and crazy behavior. You're finally getting rid of her. At least for a while."

"I didn't say anything!" Cody said, posturing defensively.

But that little smile was still on his face.

"Just for the record, Cody, this changes nothing. I will never—repeat, *never*—go out with you. You got that?"

The sides of his face pointing upward fell and headed south.

Island Food & Spirits
by
Hayley Powell

I ran into an old high-school friend, Beth Leighton, at this year's Hayseed Ball, who just happened to be in town visiting her parents. I hadn't seen Beth since graduation. She missed our ten-year reunion because she was building homes for orphans in Guatemala, which completely trumped my bake sale to raise funds for my daughter's sixth-grade class trip to Quebec. Beth always had this admirable knack for helping those in need. But I am proud to say that I was the one who helped Beth in a major, life-changing way. That's right. I was responsible for putting Beth on a path to her destiny and meeting and marrying her current (and fingers crossed) only husband!

We were around twenty years old at the time, and I was having quite a difficult time deciding what to do after completing just one year of college. Let's just say, studying wasn't my forte, and the only thing I really learned that year was how to become a good downhill skier. So I ended up back where I started, in my hometown of Bar Harbor, taking a year off to find myself. Which is code for goofing off and partying with my other peers, who were also "finding themselves."

I got a lucky break when out of nowhere I was asked by a wealthy summer family, who owned a fancy restaurant in town where I waited tables between my junior and senior year of high school, if I would be willing to live in their oceanfront mansion for the winter until they found a replacement caretaker who would take over in the spring. (Their regular caretaker of thirty years had recently retired to a sunnier climate.) I, of course, jumped at the chance to earn some spending money and live on my own without my mother monitoring my comings and goings.

It was a cushy gig. Basically, I just had to live there from September to March and make sure everything was in working order and not let the pipes freeze up over the winter. I was the envy of all my friends. As they headed back to those tiny dorm rooms at college, I was going to be living the high life in a multimillion-dollar estate. Granted, I was told to live in the maid's quarters; but still, it was better than my bedroom at my mother's house, which still sported a ladybug phone and an 'N Sync poster on the wall.

It was a glamorous life spent sipping wine on the porch and watching the leaves change color. But by November, the novelty had worn off. I missed my friends and was bored out of my mind. My closest gal pals had planned a Fort Lauderdale Thanksgiving weekend getaway, but I was unable to attend because of my caretaking duties. I was totally bummed.

By Christmas, I was climbing the walls. I was pretty much over this cold prison by the sea. And to make matters worse, I began hearing strange noises in the night. Squeaks and creaks and all kinds of rustling sounds. Great. Just what I needed. A haunted house. One night I woke up to eerie laughter. Was it a ghost? No, I had just fallen asleep with the TV on and it was a studio audience laughing at David Letterman's joke. The weird sounds persisted, however, and I checked every nook and cranny in the house, even the cobwebbed attic, which was downright creepy. But I didn't find anything. Maybe it was just squirrels running around on top of the roof.

Finally, during the Christmas break, my best friends since kindergarten——Liddy, Mona, Beth,

Annette, and Penny—descended on the mansion one night for an evening of gorging on our favorite comfort food, including my mother's famous chocolate pudding recipe she used to whip up when my girlfriends came over to the house. Liddy came armed with spirits just for the occasion—the good kind of spirits, not the ones apparently roaming around in this big house. Her spirits included top-shelf gin she swiped from her parents.

It was just like our high-school sleepovers, in our cute pj's, with lots of gossiping and giggling. But pretty soon those bizarre scratching noises coming from somewhere inside the house started up again. Mona said it sounded like a dog's toenails on the hardwood floors. Suddenly a horrible shrieking noise echoed through the house and all five of us jumped up off the floor, screaming, as we piled onto the couch. We huddled together as the terrifying shrieks stopped and started all over again. Nobody knew what to do.

As usual, in any kind of crisis, my bladder was ready to burst; but the bathroom was down the long hallway, exactly where the frightening noises were coming from. Beth, always helping those in need, agreed to accompany me.

The rest of the girls watched, barely breathing, as Beth and I made our way to the bathroom. Beth slowly opened the door and I felt along the wall for the light switch, when suddenly our eyes settled on the grotesque face of a monster in the bathroom illuminated by the moonlight through the window. We both screamed bloody murder! My finger finally found the switch; the lights snapped on; we found ourselves face-to-face with a giant raccoon standing on top of the closed toilet seat. It was screeching and it wasn't alone. The bathroom was overrun with the wild creatures. Hearing our screams, Liddy went into survival mode and ran to push the panic button on the alarm system, which was wired to the police station in town.

Now I have previously mentioned how quiet the town of Bar Harbor is in the middle of winter. Nothing much ever happens; so when a call does come in, both the police and the fire department respond with flashing squad cars and wailing fire trucks. Then there are the ten to fifteen volunteer police and firemen, bored at home, glued to their police scanners, eager to tag along in the unlikely event they're needed.

Well, when the whole posse arrived, they found five screaming, babbling girls all shouting at the same time about a pack of wild animals in the bathroom. The police chief just stood there taking in the empty gin bottle on the coffee table and the five of us decked out in our fancy pj's. No further explanation seemed necessary.

As it turned out, there was only one mother raccoon and three baby ones, which were quickly trapped and carried away. We never found out how they got in, but one of the babies must have accidentally pushed against the bathroom door, locking the whole brood inside.

The police chief mercifully never mentioned the gin bottle. He just told us to stay put for the evening. During all the commotion, Beth struck up a conversation with one of the volunteer policemen, Danny Mays, who recently had relocated to Bar Harbor from Belfast. Well, before the raccoons were deposited back into the wild, they had planned the first of many dates, which would eventually lead to their wedding, with a rousing reception at the Kebo Valley Golf Club, less than two years later. Yes, if I hadn't decided to become a caretaker for the winter, Beth might never have met her future husband. That's me. I love helping people.

Now if you have a sweet tooth like me, I probably lost you at my mother's chocolate pudding recipe. I have a craving too, so let's make some together. And nothing goes better with chocolate than a chilled glass of champagne.

Pomegranate Champagne Cocktail

Ingredients

1 ounce chilled pomegranate juice

3 ounces your favorite chilled champagne

Pour the pomegranate juice into a champagne flute, then top with the champagne. Grab some chocolate, and sit back and relax!

Mom's Chocolate Pudding

Ingredients

1/3 cup sugar

1/4 cup cocoa powder

3 tablespoons cornstarch

1/8 teaspoon salt

2 cups milk

1 teaspoon vanilla extract

In a microwavable bowl, combine your first four ingredients. Stir in the milk until smooth. Microwave, uncovered on high for three minutes. Microwave at one-minute intervals, stirring after each minute until thick and creamy. Stir in the vanilla. Pour into a bowl and refrigerate. Spoon into bowls and add fresh whipped topping if desired and then dig in!

Chapter 27

As she rushed to the office after calling Sergio, Hayley realized that during all the commotion after the shooting, she had failed to nail down the identity of Cody's secret paramour. He certainly wasn't talking about his red-hot affair, despite Hayley's threats to expose the affair to his unbalanced other half. And he was probably reasonably confident, given what happened at the shore path, that Hayley would steer clear of his batty, gun-toting wife.

There was always e-mail.

At this point Kerry Donovan was completely convinced Hayley was the other woman, so it would be a challenge convincing her otherwise.

Hayley arrived at the *Island Times* over an hour late. She shed her coat and quietly made a beeline for her desk, but she wasn't fast enough.

Sal charged out from the back bull pen to the

front office. He was so incensed that Hayley could almost see smoke coming out of his ears, like some Looney Tunes character who ate a burrito with too much hot sauce.

"Hayley, I told you to investigate Bessie Winthrop's death on your own time! So now you owe me an extra hour's work!" Sal bellowed.

"I'm only late because I've been working on a *huge* crime story for Bruce's column," Hayley said.

"What huge crime story?"

"A local shooting."

"What? Why didn't you say so?"

"You didn't give me a chance."

"Who got shot?"

"Me. Well, as you can see, I didn't get shot. The gunman didn't have very good aim."

"You? Why am I not surprised?"

"That's exactly what Sergio said. Why does everybody think I attract trouble?"

Sal opened his mouth to respond, but Hayley held a hand up, stopping him. "Don't answer that."

"Any info on the shooter?"

Hayley nodded. "Cody Donovan's wife. Honestly, I don't think she was out to hurt us. I think she just wanted to scare us."

"*Us?*"

"I was with Cody at the time."

"I see."

Hayley looked at Sal's face.

Smug.

Full of judgment.

"No, Sal. I am *not* fooling around with Cody Donovan!"

"Apparently, his wife seems to think so."

"Well, she's wrong! There is *nothing* going on between us!"

"So what were you doing with him?"

Hayley took a deep breath. "I was questioning him for a story."

"What story?"

Checkmate.

He would find out eventually.

"Bessie Winthrop's death."

Sal folded his beefy arms and smiled. "You owe me an hour's work."

"But, Sal—"

"Just because another crime just happened to occur while you were working on the Bessie story doesn't get you off the hook. Where's Mrs. Donovan now?"

"I'm assuming she's handcuffed and in the back of Sergio's cruiser. He was heading over to arrest her after I called him twenty minutes ago."

"Okay, write it up. I want it posted online before the *Herald* scoops us. I'm sure they've already heard about it on the police scanner."

Hayley fired up her desktop computer and began to type furiously as the door to the office swung open. A statuesque, elegant woman in her early fifties swept inside.

It was Eliza Richards.

The mayor of Bar Harbor.

"Hello, Hayley. You ready, Sal?"

Sal nodded, a goofy grin on his face.

His crush on her was painfully obvious.

"We're just doing a quick interview over b-breakfast," Sal stammered.

"You don't have to explain anything to me, Sal. I'm not your wife," Hayley said, smiling as she watched Sal squirm a little. It was as if he was afraid she could see the impure thoughts pulsing through his brain.

"I just don't want people talking about us," Sal said, laughing, and then quickly stopping himself so he didn't sound like an idiot.

Too late.

"I'm sure you're in the clear, Sal," Hayley said. "You look lovely today, Mayor Richards."

"Why, thank you, Hayley," the mayor giggled, touching her hair to make sure every strand was in its proper place.

Mayor Richards was indeed a classy broad, a fashion plate with an impeccable style that most women in town looked up to and admired.

Except for Liddy, who refused to be impressed, given the fact she saw herself as the number one clotheshorse in town. That was why she refused to vote for Mayor Richards.

Sal couldn't help himself. He had to explain everything in case this little midmorning confab was misconstrued and got back to his wife. "We're going to the coffee shop across the street. I want to ask the mayor some questions about her efforts to overhaul the town's parking spaces and make them diagonal so the streets can accommodate more vehicles, given the fact over a million tourists pour into town every summer!"

"Thank you for that detailed rundown of your agenda at the coffee shop, Sal," Hayley said, teasing him.

"The old-school city council members are fighting it, of course," the mayor said. "They want to veto any change! But change is good. I just need to get the public on my side, especially the ones with local businesses who depend on a lot of tourists showing up every year."

Hayley noticed a little spittle glistening on the sides of Sal's mouth.

He was literally drooling.

Sal cleared his throat and wiped his mouth. "Well, we better be going."

Hayley stood up from her desk, noticing a beautiful and bedazzling bracelet on the mayor's wrist. "Oh, that's gorgeous."

"Isn't it?" the mayor cooed, glancing over to

Sal, who nodded vigorously, like a bashful, horny teenage boy.

"What is that? Some kind of flower?" Hayley asked, pointing to the center of the bracelet.

"It's a gold poppy bangle. A one of a kind. Made specially for me by a jeweler in France I met while on holiday there a few years ago."

"It's very unique."

And yet very familiar.

Hayley was sure she had seen it before.

And then it hit her.

Like a ton of bricks.

Gold poppy bangle.

Hayley let go of the mayor's hand and casually came around her desk and reached into her bag, which was hanging on the coatrack by its strap. She covertly pulled out the photos she had printed off Bessie's phone and studied them for a moment.

The mysterious, unseen woman in bed with Cody was wearing the exact same bracelet.

She glanced over at the bracelet the mayor was wearing.

Gold poppy bangle.

Polished band of sterling silver.

One of a kind.

The other woman Cody was sleeping with was the mayor of Bar Harbor.

Sal came up behind Hayley, reaching for his winter jacket and bumped into Hayley. She fell forward, grabbing the coatrack to steady herself, and dropped the pictures. They scattered across the floor.

Most of them faceup.

Hayley pounced on them and frantically began scooping them up, but she just wasn't fast enough.

The mayor stared at the photos.

Her face frozen.

There was no mistaking what they were.

And who was in them.

Sal was too busy struggling into his coat to notice.

Mayor Richards calmly turned to Sal as Hayley stuffed the photos back inside her bag. "Do you mind if I meet you at the coffee shop? I have some business to take care of first."

"Sure. I'll order you an English breakfast tea with honey. I know how you like that with your poppy seed lemon muffin," Sal said, winking at the mayor as he shuffled out the door.

The second the door shut, the mayor swung around to face Hayley. "Please, Hayley, I'm begging you. Please don't tell anyone. I'm up for reelection in November."

"I'm not out to create a scandal. I just—"

"I don't know where you got those, but, trust me, it was a brief affair. Nothing consequential. A mindless fling. One I regret with all my heart. It's over, and I promise I will never stray again."

"That's nice, but I'm not interested in exposing—"

"My husband is a good man. He loves me. Our thirtieth wedding anniversary is around the corner. If he were ever to find out—"

"Mayor Richards, you have to believe, I don't plan on saying anything to anyone. If you are up front and honest with me."

"Of course. Why wouldn't I be?"

"Well, you are sneaking around behind your husband's back. And then there is the fact that you are a politician."

Mayor Richards grimaced.

"I have to ask. Did you have anything to do with Bessie Winthrop's death?"

"Bessie? I thought she died of a heart attack. Isn't that what the papers said?"

"Yes, but I happen to think there is more to the story, and you're smack in the middle of it."

"I barely knew Bessie. Why would I do anything to harm her? Good Lord, Hayley, I went to Brown. I did time in the Peace Corps. I support our troops. How can you even insinuate I would do anything so insidious? How could anyone think that?"

The mayor was speaking passionately, but her eyes were telling a different story.

She was scared.

Worried.

Purposefully vague.

"Because Bessie was the one who took these

pictures," Hayley said. "And I get the feeling you're not being forthright with me about barely knowing her."

"It's true. I knew her name, but we hardly spoke," the mayor said, eyes downcast, "until Cody told me she was blackmailing him. I was shocked. I had no idea she had been following us around. But it didn't matter that Cody was sleeping with the mayor of Bar Harbor. She was only interested in him approving her bank loan. I begged Cody to give her anything she wanted, but he was resistant. So I went to her house to offer her money for her business if she gave her assurances that my name would never be dragged into a scandal."

"So you were going to bribe her into keeping quiet about the affair?"

"When you put it that way, it sounds so unseemly. But I suppose you're right."

"Did Bessie agree?"

"I never had the chance to make my offer. When I pulled up in front of her house, she was on the front lawn talking to someone else."

"Who is it she was talking to?"

"I forget his name, but he didn't look happy. He was shouting at her. It was getting very heated. I don't know what happened after that, because I was afraid they would see me, so I drove away."

"So you know the man?"

"Yes. The vet. I can't remember his name. I don't keep pets."

"Dr. Winston?"

"No. I know Dr. Winston. He's been around for years. We served on the school board together. No, it was the new one—the one who replaced Dr. Winston."

"Dr. Palmer?"

"Yes, that's the one. It was him. Dr. Palmer."

Chapter 28

"Oh, Hayley, I'm so sorry. I was really hoping it would work out with him, " Liddy said, sipping her piping-hot Baileys Irish Cream and coffee.

"It was pretty much over at the Hayseed Ball," Hayley said.

"So the cute doctor is a brutal killer. Gotta admit, I didn't see that one coming," Mona said, chugging her beer.

The three of them were sitting side by side on stools at Drinks Like A Fish. Hayley met her two besties for cocktails after she got off work, which was an hour later than usual, since she had to put in that extra time for being late.

"Mayor Richards just saw them talking," Hayley said. "Maybe he was making a house call. Bessie had something like seventeen cats."

"Don't try putting a positive spin on it. He killed her," Mona said, slamming her Coors Light down on the bar and waving at Michelle, the bartender, to fetch her another.

"You don't know that," Hayley said.

"Mona's right. It's always the handsome, flawless, square-jawed, heroic-looking romantic interest whom no one suspects. You gotta have the twist ending!" Liddy cried.

"So, what should I do?"

"I have an idea," Liddy said, spinning around on her stool to face her friends.

"I never like it when Liddy has one of her big ideas," Mona replied, groaning.

"Too bad, Mona. Because it involves you and that scruffy, ungroomed mutt of yours, Bagpipes."

"Bagley. His name is Bagley, and he's not a mutt. He's a komondor," Mona retorted.

"Who cares? That Hungarian shepherd dog with the chronic flea problem, which is the chief reason, by the way, I never step foot inside your house," Liddy said. "Well, that and the fact you have a bazillion kids and there is bound to be head lice."

"Get to the point, Liddy."

"I say we swing by Mona's house and pick up her dog, and then show up at Dr. Palmer's office to see if he has a cream or a spray or something he can prescribe to alleviate poor Bagpipes' itchiness."

"Bagley," Mona said through gritted teeth.

"Hayley already has used Leroy and Blueberry as decoys," Liddy said, ignoring her. "If they show up again, it's bound to arouse suspicion. We'll have to use Bagpipes. Just keep him away from me. God knows what else is living underneath that mangy coat of fur."

"Bagley!" Mona shrieked. "And it's an awful idea!"

"No, it just might work," Hayley said, her mind racing.

"Two against one," Mona groused. "It's always two against one."

Within twenty minutes Mona was carrying Bagley underneath her arm, depositing the dog on top of the reception desk at Dr. Palmer's clinic. Hayley and Liddy hung back by the door to the waiting area as Mona slowly explained why her dog needed to be examined.

Marla Heasley, Dr. Palmer's perky assistant, scratched Bagley's head. "Fleas, huh? Well, the doctor is out right now, and I'm not sure when he will be back."

"As you can see, the poor thing is very distressed from all the itching and scratching," Mona said.

Bagley licked Marla's face, panting, smiling, jowls flapping.

"I think he's handling the discomfort just fine," Marla said, not the least bit suspicious, "but let me take him in the back until the doctor returns. In the meantime you can fill out some paperwork. Come with me, Bagley."

Marla led Bagley out through a door into another room in the back of the clinic. The happy dog trotted loyally behind her, tail wagging.

"Why doesn't he obey *me* like that?" Mona asked, perusing the papers.

"What is it with her and animals? They all seem to love her. Frankly, I don't see it," Hayley said, annoyed.

"If she comes back, Mona, give us a signal," Liddy said, pretending she was in a John le Carré novel.

"Like what? Smoke signals?"

Liddy sighed. "Just text me from your phone, okay?"

"Liddy, I'm not so sure this is a good idea . . . ," Hayley said.

Liddy grabbed Hayley by the hand and dragged her into Dr. Palmer's office, which was to the right of the reception area in the opposite direction from where Marla escorted Bagley.

They looked around before setting their sights on the desktop computer with a large, flat-screen monitor.

Liddy sat down and began clicking on all the files.

"Liddy, I have a bad feeling about this——"

"Would you relax? We're not going to get caught. Now where should I start first?"

"Marla keeps a detailed calendar of all the doctor's appointments. Maybe we can see if he met Bessie more than just that one time."

Liddy nodded and opened the calendar program. She scrolled down the days, the weeks, the months.

"Look at all the times he went to the gym. At least we've solved 'The Mystery of the Six-Pack Abs,'" Liddy said, impressed.

Hayley pulled the keyboard away from Liddy and typed Bessie into the search engine of the calendar program.

"He met with Bessie on three occasions. And look at what he typed in the notes column from the meeting. 'Last warning.' What was he warning her about?"

"Beats me. But Mr. Perfect is hiding something. I can feel it," Liddy said.

Hayley heard a buzzing sound. "What's that?"

"What?"

Another buzzing sound.

"Don't you hear that?"

"Oh, it's just my phone," Liddy said. "We're in the middle of a spy operation here. Whoever it is, I can call that person back."

"But didn't you tell Mona to text you if something was wrong?"

Liddy gulped, suddenly realizing that, and grabbed the phone out of her pocket.

She read the text.

"What does it say?"

"He's back."

"Dr. Palmer?"

Liddy nodded.

"We have to get out of here before he comes in and finds us."

"Too late," Liddy mouthed to Hayley.

Hayley pivoted to see Dr. Palmer standing in the doorway.

He did not look happy to see them.

Chapter 29

"I'm calling the police!" Marla screeched as she poked her head over Aaron's shoulder as he stood in the doorway.

Aaron turned to her. "No, Marla, no one's calling the police."

"But, Dr. Palmer, they can't just burst in here and rifle through your files. That's against the law and they should be arrested!"

Aaron took Marla's hands into his own and squeezed.

She swooned, and the hard look on her face instantly melted.

"I'm guessing Ms. Powell and her friend—"

"Liddy Crawford," Liddy cooed, batting her eyes, struck by the doctor's good looks.

"Nice to meet you. I'm guessing Ms. Powell and Ms. Crawford were just being overzealous in their pursuit of justice."

He made their breaking-and-entering attempt sound almost noble.

God, he was sexy.

"Pursuit of what? I don't understand," Marla huffed. "I really think I should call Chief Alvares and get him down here. This woman has clearly been trying to insinuate herself into your life for nefarious reasons. It's a good thing we found out now before you opened your heart and she stomped on it. You need someone who would rather be dragged along the ground, tied to the back of a speeding pickup truck, than do anything that would make you unhappy, . . ."

Aaron held his hand up in front of her. "Okay, Marla, I want you to stop and take a deep breath for me."

Marla obediently followed his instructions, mesmerized by his penetrating eyes.

"That's good. Now hold it a minute and release," he said, still holding her hands.

Marla let out a *whoosh* of air.

"Feel better?"

She nodded.

"Good. Now there are a couple of pet owners out in reception still filling out paperwork. Why don't you go check on their progress?"

"Yes, Dr. Palmer," Marla said, with a fawning smile, spinning around like Julie Andrews in the Swiss Alps, and floating back out front.

Aaron watched her go; then he turned back to

Hayley and Mona. "Am I right to assume this has something to do with Bessie Winthrop?"

Hayley nodded.

Liddy stepped forward and smiled brightly at the doctor. "I'm surprised at you, Hayley. How could you think this tall hunk of a man could possibly have done anything sordid? One look into those gorgeous eyes will tell you the man is completely innocent."

"I never said I thought you did it," Hayley tried to explain to Aaron, who was still not smiling.

"Then what are you doing in my office, on my computer?" Aaron asked, stepping into the office and closing the door.

"As you know, I've been conducting my own little investigation, trying to prove that there was more to Bessie's death than clogged arteries—"

"I'm aware of that, Hayley. I was with you at the Garbers' house when you decided to tear apart their bedroom, looking for evidence to connect them to this so-called crime."

"Yes, well, recently I came in contact with someone who saw you having an argument with Bessie on her front lawn before she died."

"That someone was Mayor Richards, I presume?"

"Yes. How did you know?"

"It was hard to miss her. She was gawking at us for so long as she drove by the house that she almost drove her Volvo right into a telephone pole."

"So it's true? You were arguing with Bessie?"

"Yes," Aaron said matter-of-factly.

Liddy moaned. She wasn't quite ready to face the fact that Dr. Palmer was anything but Mr. Perfect in the flesh.

"I was making a house call. One of Bessie's cats was hiding under the couch and not eating. Turns out the cat was pregnant. Just what that household needed. More cats. As I left, I scolded Bessie for having too many pets. The condition of her house was unsanitary. It was an unhealthy environment for her *and* the cats. I told her she needed to find other homes for some of them. She didn't take kindly to me telling her what to do. She just blew up at me."

"Yes, Bessie did have a temper," Hayley said. "So that's what you were talking about when you said you were giving her a last warning?"

"I told her if she refused to take action, I was going to be forced to call animal control. That's when she really went nuts. I barely got out of there with my life."

"I see," Hayley said, suddenly feeling foolish.

"You could've just called me up and asked me, instead of breaking into my office," Aaron said.

"That's what *I* told her," Liddy said, before turning her head sideways and then whispering to Hayley, "I figure you've already blown it, so maybe I have a chance."

"So you honestly thought I was capable of murder?" Aaron asked. There was a sad, disappointed look on his face.

Hayley suddenly knew what Marla was talking about. She would rather be dragged through the streets, tied to the back of a pickup truck, than see that hurt look again.

Her phone buzzed and she yanked it out of her jeans pocket.

It was a text from Sal.

Another break-in at pharmacy. Get over there now.

Hayley looked up at Aaron. "I'm sorry. I have to go. It's a work thing."

Aaron nodded. "Okay. See you around."

It sounded like he didn't mean it.

"I have nowhere to go," Liddy said. "I can stay."

"I'm afraid I have some work to do. Like your friend Mona's dog. The flea problem? She's outside waiting. Unless that was just an excuse to come over here."

"No, trust me. That's real. They're going to have to put a tent over Mona's house," Liddy said as Aaron opened the door to his office and ushered them out.

Hayley stopped and opened her mouth to say something to Aaron, but nothing came out. He gave her a slight nod and a thin smile. She felt silly, just standing there with her mouth hanging open, so she kept going. She walked out of the vet's office and never looked back.

It was a short walk down Cottage Street to the pharmacy. Liddy spent the entire time apologizing for inappropriately hitting on Hayley's man. Hayley explained that he wasn't her man. There was nothing between them, so Liddy should absolutely go for it. Liddy veered off to Drinks Like A Fish to pick up her car, and Hayley continued on to the pharmacy. A squad car was parked out front, with the blue lights flashing. Hayley entered to find the pharmacist on duty, Jimmy MacDonald, being interviewed by Officers Donnie and Earl, two young local cops with reputations for being, well, young and wet behind the ears when it came to police work.

So wet they were almost drowning.

Hayley waited patiently for the officers to finish with their questioning and start writing out a report.

Jimmy noticed Hayley and waved her over.

"You covering this for the paper, Hayley?"

"Yeah, how's it going, Jimmy?"

Jimmy MacDonald was in his sixties, born and raised in Bar Harbor, a retired fireman who wasn't ready to spend the rest of his life fishing and arguing politics, so he went back to school for his

PharmD and now worked the late shift at the local pharmacy.

"Not too good," Jimmy said, wiping his sweaty hands on his white lab coat.

"Mind if I ask you a few questions now that Crockett and Tubbs are done?"

Jimmy snickered and shook his head. "Idiots. I don't know why Chief Alvares puts up with them."

Officers Donnie and Earl were bickering with each other while leaning over the checkout counter, trying to fill out the report.

"What was taken?" Hayley asked.

"OxyContin. What else? I know it's a couple of tweaked-out teenagers who ran out of Robitussin to chug and decided to kick it up a notch and grab some stash from here while I was in the back filling a prescription."

"Did you get a look at them?"

"No, like I told the cops, they were gone before I knew they were even here. The only reason I noticed anything missing is because they knocked over a Tylenol display when they were running away."

Hayley jotted everything down on a notepad she kept in her jacket breast pocket.

"I thought working in a pharmacy would be calm and relaxing after thirty years of running into burning buildings, but I tell you, Hayley, there's more stress here than you can imagine. I never took into account all the crazy people I've had to deal with on a daily basis."

"I hear you, Jimmy."

"Believe me, I know *everybody's* secrets," he said, cackling. "And I mean everybody's. Let's go out for a drink sometime and I'll fill you in. Some of the stories will haunt you in your sleep."

"Isn't that unethical?"

"Sure. But I could give a crap. I'm old. What can they do to me?"

Hayley laughed. "Well, if you remember anything else, Jimmy, be sure to give me a call. And I will take you up on that drink."

Hayley turned to go.

Officers Donnie and Earl were now fighting over the police report itself. One trying to grab it from the other. Both probably wanting to hand it to the chief personally. It tore in half.

And then they argued over that.

Hayley turned back to Jimmy. "Did you ever wait on Bessie Winthrop?"

"Of course. That one wasn't just crazy. She was *professionally* crazy, if you know what I mean."

"I do know. I was friends with Bessie. She certainly was colorful."

"Don't get me wrong. I liked the broad. She never cut the line or yelled if her heart medication wasn't ready. And she liked me because I bought a box of chocolates from her. They were awful. I dumped the box after trying just one. But I never said anything to her. Why not stay on her good side? In fact, she came in here on the day she died and asked if I wanted to buy another box. I said sure. Mostly because I felt sorry for her. But I never got it. She died that night."

"How did she seem that day? Did you notice anything out of the ordinary?"

"No, not really. She seemed pretty normal. I mean, for Bessie. She just picked up her medication and then they left."

"*They*? She was with someone?"

"Yeah, a lady."

"Do you know who she is?"

"Not by name, but I've seen her around town. I think she owns a catering business or something."

"Nina Foster-Jones?"

"Yeah, that's the one. I see her ads in the paper all the time. She wears that tacky smiley-face apron and the matching chef's hat, and she's holding a wooden spoon in the air."

"Are you sure they walked in here *together*?"

"Yeah, I'm pretty sure."

"I know for a fact they didn't like each other. Could you sense any kind of tension between them?"

"No, not at all. In fact, I heard her say to Bessie that everything was going to be all right, and she would take care of everything."

"Take care of what?"

"Beats me. I handed Bessie her bag and then they left."

"*Together?* You're absolutely sure?"

Jimmy nodded.

Bessie and Nina detested each other. Nina was threatening legal action against Bessie for stealing her ideas. What were they doing hanging around each other? And what was Nina going to take care of for Bessie?

Hayley felt a charge of excitement.

She finally had a new lead to follow.

And it led straight to Bessie's archrival, Nina Foster-Jones.

Chapter 30

Nina Foster-Jones was a realist. She wasn't going to become a Food Network star over night. It was going to take a lot of hard work, perseverance, and a large stack of applications to various cable-TV-network cooking-competition shows. Her catering business did decent-enough business during the summer months, but she was still just getting by and unable to bank enough money to get her through the harsh winter months.

She was still anxiously awaiting her big break. With a mortgage to pay and mounting credit card debt from buying all of the top-brand cooking utensils and pots and pans, not to mention an expensive wardrobe for her own YouTube cooking instruction videos, Nina had little choice but to find a "day job."

When Gretchen Maxwell finally retired from the local branch of Grand Future Insurance after slipping on a patch of ice and breaking her hip in

January, Nina swooped in and applied for her job. Nina had zero interest in overseeing insurance policies; but it was a steady paycheck, and it would go a long way in paying the monthly minimum interest on her Visa bill.

Hayley entered the office of Grand Future Insurance, on the second floor of a building next to the post office on Cottage Street. The receptionist pointed Hayley toward Nina's tiny office in the back, not bothering even to call Nina to let her know she had a visitor. Just a handful of people worked in this tiny satellite office of the main corporate headquarters in Chicago.

Nina's door was open, and she was behind her desk, feet up, flipping through the latest issue of *Bon Appétit* magazine.

"Nina?"

The sound of Hayley's voice startled her, and she almost tipped over in her chair as she swung her feet off the desk, nearly knocking a lamp over. She hastily crammed the magazine into her oversize turquoise purse, which was on the floor.

"Hayley, you scared the stuffing out of me!" Nina said, resting her hand over her heart. "Which reminds me, I have a new cranberry-and-walnut stuffing recipe you'll just die over. Make sure I give it to you before you leave. Maybe you can write about it in your column. Just don't forget to give me the credit."

"Will do, Nina. But this month I'm doing all chocolate recipes in honor of Valentine's Day."

"Okay. I will e-mail you my chocolate strawberry cream-cheese tart recipe. Three words. Better. Than. Sex."

"Sounds delicious."

"It's a religious experience. Frankly, I'm surprised you don't give me more credit in that cute little column of yours. I've noticed on more than one occasion you borrowed heavily from my blog."

"I'm sorry, Nina, I've never read your blog."

Nina chortled. "Oh, come on, Hayley. You can admit it. I won't sue."

"That's not what Bessie Winthrop told me."

Nina's face reddened and suddenly she was all business. "Now, are you here to discuss your policy? Being relatively new here, I'm not familiar with what you have covered with us, but if you just give me a minute to bring up your file on the computer, I'll get myself up to speed."

"Actually, I'm not here to talk about *my* policy."

"Oh?"

"I'm here about Bessie Winthrop."

"You really should've made an appointment. It's very busy around here today."

Hayley looked outside the office door.

It was so quiet she was half expecting a tumbleweed to blow past.

"This will only take a second, Nina."

"I know all about you, Hayley. I've heard the

stories. Running all over town, pointing fingers at people like some ambulance-chasing lawyer, accusing every last local of engaging in some treacherous deed. Well, it won't work with me. My hands are clean. I had nothing to do with Bessie's murder."

"So you think it *was* a murder? Because Sabrina Merryweather remains convinced Bessie died of heart disease. That's interesting."

"Oh no. Don't you even start insinuating that I know more than I do. I have my professional reputation to protect! If you even dare whisper a false accusation, I *will* sue you. Because we both know what's really going on here."

"We do?"

"Yes. You are threatened by my success."

"Success"?

Her greatest claim to fame was catering a party at the rented house of eighties teen pop star Debbie Gibson two summers ago.

"I'm on the cusp of fame. That's right, Hayley, the cusp. I am *this* close to a major break. And I know you are seething with jealousy, and are hoping to bring me down so you can capitalize on those precious food-and-cocktails columns of yours. Well, you can't stop me! I will be taking my rightful place as the lead-in show to Rachael Ray on the Food Network!"

This woman is bananas.

"I'm not interested in competing with you, Nina.

I'm happy just writing my column and raising my kids here in little ole Bar Harbor!"

"Bull puckey! Who on earth would be satisfied just doing that?"

Nina assumed everybody had her breadth of ambition.

She couldn't have been more wrong.

"Just answer one question, and I promise to steer clear of your path to stardom."

"What?"

"If you and Bessie were such bitter rivals, why were you hanging around together on the day she died?"

"I don't know what you're talking about."

"Jimmy MacDonald saw the two of you at the pharmacy and you seemed quite friendly. In fact, he overheard you tell Bessie not to worry, you'd take care of everything. What did you mean by that?"

"Is that what this is all about? Good Lord, Hayley, Bessie and I weren't girlfriends. We didn't pal around together. We just happened to run into each other outside the pharmacy as we were going in. She asked if we could call a truce for two minutes so she could ask me a professional question."

"What kind of professional question?"

"She knew I had recently replaced Gretchen Maxwell at Grand Future Insurance. Bessie had a life insurance policy with us."

"Life insurance?"

Alarm bells went off in Hayley's head.

"Yes. She recently made a change to her policy and so she just wanted me to make sure the revisions were processed and completed."

"Did she change the name of the beneficiary?"

"I'm sorry, Hayley, I can't divulge that information. It would be a breach of professional ethics."

"Oh, come on, Nina. Give me a hint."

"I could get fired, Hayley, and then how would I pay for my YouTube videos? I can't slip up now. *Cusp, Hayley!* Do you hear me? I'm on the *cusp*!"

Hayley knew she wasn't going to get any more out of the future Food Network superstar.

Believe it or not, a small part of Hayley was rooting for her to make it.

Someone who wanted something so badly, and was willing to work her tail off to get it, at least deserved a little success.

But no matter how much fame and fortune followed, Hayley suspected Nina Foster-Jones would still be just as paranoid and petty and unhappy as she was now.

Chapter 31

Hayley knew she couldn't call Sergio to rustle up a warrant in order to get a peek at Bessie's life insurance policy at Grand Future Insurance. Mostly because there was no active murder investigation at this point, and the police, the coroner, and the entire town were still convinced Bessie's heart just gave out.

So if Bessie had kept a copy of her policy, it would most likely still be inside the house somewhere.

And Hayley still had the key.

Her previous search was cut short by Mary Garber calling the police, so she knew she had to be more careful this time, and not be spotted by a nosy neighbor or passerby.

Hayley parked her car at the far end of the street and sat there, engine idling, watching the neighborhood, waiting for her opportunity to slip inside Bessie's house undetected.

She was there about ten minutes when Mary Garber slammed out of her house, cupping her hands and blowing into them to keep warm before climbing into her Jeep Cherokee. It took a few tries before the Jeep's engine sputtered to life. Mary backed out of the driveway and passed Hayley's car, not even noticing her. Mary's eyes were clear and focused, which was unusual, since most of the time she was blistering drunk. Hayley thought perhaps she might be on a mission to the liquor store.

Hayley got out of her car and scurried down the street to Bessie's house. She plucked the key from her pocket and inserted it into the lock; but when she turned the knob, the door creaked open.

The house was already unlocked.

Hayley guardedly stepped inside, trying not to make any sound; she looked around.

The house appeared to be just as she had last seen it.

Like a bomb had hit it.

Lots of clutter and that unrelenting odor.

Hayley glanced around. She had done a pretty thorough sweep of the downstairs and Bessie's bedroom before she got caught by Sergio.

But she never made it to that upstairs storage closet.

She slowly walked up the steps, past the closed

door to Bessie's bedroom, before stopping at the hallway closet.

She opened it and a stack of cookbooks and stuffed file folders came tumbling down off the top shelf, nearly burying Hayley alive.

She got down on her knees and started sifting through all the strewn junk. Mostly copied old fan letters to Bessie's childhood idol, Julia Child, and more current kitchen masters like that grouchy, loud Gordon Ramsay and that cackling, butter-loving Paula Deen.

And then there were recipes.

Scores of scraps of paper where Bessie scribbled new spins on old-time favorites, like bread pudding and lemon squares.

After a few minutes of sorting through the different folders, Hayley happened upon one unlabeled folder stuffed with reams of paper.

She fanned through it.

An overdue fire insurance premium.

A last warning for her car insurance payment.

This had to be it.

Hayley kept skimming through the papers.

The bank threatening to foreclose on her house if she didn't pay her mortgage.

A letter to her health insurance company begging them to reduce her co-payment for her heart medication.

About halfway through the stack, Hayley identified the logo for Grand Future Insurance.

She speedily read through the five pages stapled together.

It was definitely the policy Nina was talking about.

Near the bottom of the last page, the name "Tawnia Wentworth" was listed as the primary beneficiary.

Tawnia Wentworth.

Why did Hayley know that name?

Of course!

Tawnia was sixteen years old and in Gemma's class in high school. She lived with her mother, Nancy, who was divorced from Rand Winthrop, Bessie's estranged brother. Rand had blown town years ago when Tawnia was not even three years old because he felt stifled by the responsibilities of marriage and fatherhood. Hayley last heard he was working on a dude ranch in Wyoming.

Bessie despised her brother for deserting his young family and never spoke to him again, but she always had a soft spot for her niece, Tawnia, even though the two rarely saw each other.

That would make perfect sense.

But Nancy had a good job and was saving her money so Tawnia could go to college. Hayley found it hard to believe that Tawnia or her mother would commit such a heinous act over some insurance money. They may not have even been aware of the policy.

Hayley suddenly heard a thumping sound coming from the bedroom.

Her ears perked up and she knelt there on the floor, frozen.

Was someone else in the house?

The last time when she and Sergio left, Hayley distinctly remembered leaving the bedroom door open. Now it was closed.

A voice inside her was screaming, *"Get the hell out!"*

And for once, she decided to listen.

Hayley slowly stood up and moved silently down the hall toward the stairs. She was just about halfway there when the door to the bedroom swung open and a hulking man, twice Hayley's size, stepped out into the hallway, his back to her, and peered down the staircase.

He was wearing a black ski mask, black sweater, and jeans; he was listening to hear if Hayley had gone, not realizing she was now standing right behind him.

Hayley stood, terror-stricken, not daring to move a muscle.

The giant man craned his neck to get a glimpse of the foyer, which was empty. He relaxed a bit, assuming she was gone, and then turned around to head back to the bedroom.

He stopped in his tracks, thunderstruck.

The sight of the Herculean-size, masked thug

dressed in black was so spine-chilling, Hayley didn't know what else to do but let out a blood-curdling scream.

The masked man just stood there in shock for a moment, before regaining his senses and lunging at her, with muscled arms outstretched to grab her.

Hayley tried to dodge his grasp, but his massive frame blocked any room for escape. He wrapped his arms around her and picked her up off the floor, tucking her underneath one arm and jamming a meaty palm over her face to silence her screams as he carried her into the bedroom.

Hayley struggled, but she was like a newborn baby, completely helpless in his superhuman grip.

Hayley reached up with her fist and started pounding his left arm, but the muscles were so tight that he barely felt a thing. She grabbed at the sleeve of his black shirt and the fabric tore slightly, revealing a T-shaped scar on his left bicep. Before she could examine it further, the mountainous prowler let go of her mouth and opened the bedroom closet door. He tossed Hayley inside.

She hit the wall hard, and then dropped to the floor, taking down two dozen of Bessie's colorful muumuus and dresses, which were hanging on the rack.

The door slammed shut, enveloping Hayley in darkness, and then the intruder pushed something up hard against the closet, probably lodging the back of a chair underneath the knob to trap Hayley inside.

She heard him pounding away.

Hayley threw her shoulder against the door like a battering ram.

Once.

Twice.

Third time was the charm.

The chair gave way and Hayley stumbled out of the closet to freedom.

But by the time she managed to race down the stairs to the open front door, she knew the man was long gone.

Already halfway back to his beanstalk.

Chapter 32

"Oh, my God, that's so cool!" Tawnia Wentworth squealed as she shoveled air-popped popcorn into her mouth, while sitting at Hayley's kitchen table. Tawnia was dressed in baby blue sweats and a t-shirt with the teen pop princes New Direction emblazoned on it. "I mean, it's not cool that poor Aunt Bessie died, but that she was nice enough to make me the benefactory or whatever."

"Beneficiary," Gemma said, forcing a smile.

"So you had no idea you were named in Bessie's life insurance policy?"

"No! I would've been a lot nicer to her if I'd known!" Tawnia said, grabbing the saltshaker and dousing the remaining kernels in the green mixing bowl in front of her. "We hardly saw each other. She'd stop by around Christmas and give me a present, usually a gift card for Amazon or iTunes, which was so sweet of her. And when I was in the chorus of last fall's musical, *Pippin*, she was nice enough to show up at a Sunday matinee performance and give me a box of her icky chocolates, which I promptly threw away because I don't need to be getting fat like her."

Tawnia noticed both Hayley and Gemma looking aghast, so she quickly added, "God rest her soul."

Hayley stole a glance toward Gemma and mouthed "Thank you" as Tawnia dove into the bowl and scraped up the last bits of popcorn and licked them off her fingers.

Gemma nodded at her mother and then picked up the empty bowl. "I'll put another bag in the microwave."

"I'm so happy you called me to come over tonight, Gemma," Tawnia said before chugging down a glass of chocolate milk. "I mean, we rarely hang out anymore, now that we move in different social circles. It's nice to catch up."

"We're so overdue," Gemma said, her back to them, the obvious sarcasm lost on Tawnia.

But certainly not on her mother.

"So I take it Nancy didn't know about the insurance policy either?" Hayley asked.

"Mom? Are you kidding? If she had, she would've knocked off Bessie herself and bought the new Camry she's been squawking about wanting the past few months," Tawnia said, cackling, before catching herself again and forcing her face into a frown. "Poor, poor Bessie."

"So you hadn't seen her since Christmas?" Hayley asked, refilling Tawnia's glass with more chocolate milk from a plastic carton.

"Nope. She was so busy trying to start her business. No, wait. There was that one time right after New Year's when she called to ask if I would be willing to feed her cats for a couple of days while she went to New York to meet with some Food Network executives."

"She had a meeting with the Food Network?"

"Oh, God, no, but every so often she'd scrape together some money and take a bus trip down there and hang around out in front of the building, hoping to run into one of her idols, who might be willing to help her get her foot in the door. Yes, she was totally delusional."

"So you helped her out?"

"Yuck! Of course not! My mother wouldn't let me step one foot inside that house with all those nasty, disease-ridden cats. Gross! I told her no. No offense, Blackberry," Tawnia said to Blueberry, who walked past her, tail swishing.

Tawnia reached down to pet him, but Blueberry hissed and Tawnia quickly retracted her fingers.

"Was Bessie upset you refused to help her?" Hayley asked.

"She was at first, but then she got distracted. Apparently, someone was looking at her through her windows. At first, I thought she was just making it up. I mean, seriously, what kind of Peeping Tom would want to look at Aunt Bessie?"

The popcorn began popping like machine-gun fire.

Gemma stood close to the microwave, grateful that the loud noise was drowning out Tawnia's voice.

"But then Aunt Bessie saw who it was and she got really, really scared."

"Who was it?"

"Her creepy ex."

"Wolf Conway?"

"Yeah, him. What a loser. I mean, spying on Aunt Bessie? It's not like she's a Kardashian!"

"Did she open the door and confront him?"

"I don't know. I got bored and hung up."

Gemma opened the microwave door, ripped open the bag, and poured the contents into the green bowl. She walked back over to the table and put it down in front of Tawnia, who immediately scooped out a fistful and crammed it into her mouth.

"But my mother told me she had run into Bessie in the grocery store, and Bessie had told her that she had to take a restraining order out on Wolf because he wouldn't leave her alone. But that didn't stop him from showing up on her doorstep all the time. She told Mom she was really frightened that he might do something to her. He had a vicious temper, just like Aunt Bessie."

"Did your mother call the police?"

"No. Why?"

"She was family," Gemma said, trying not to slap Tawnia across the face. "Bessie was in danger."

"My daddy ditched us over twelve years ago. Mom was so mad she even made me change my last name to Wentworth, which is her maiden name. She was so done with him! She said his kooky sister is not our problem," Tawnia said coldly, before noticing the judgmental looks from Hayley and Gemma. "But, seriously, I'm sorry she's dead and all."

"Yeah, bummer about those iTunes gift certificates," Gemma said.

There was an uncomfortable silence as Tawnia realized she didn't know her audience. She slurped some more chocolate milk and then stood up from the table. "Well, I'm going to go upstairs and put some makeup on in case a couple of cute boys show up outside and throw pebbles at the window while we're doing each other's hair later."

"I'm sorry, Tawnia, but we're not going to model this slumber party after the one in *Grease,*" Gemma said.

"It's always been my fantasy having boys show up to whisk me away for a night of beer drinking and making out."

"Well, it's going to remain a fantasy, as long as you're here under my roof," Hayley said.

"I know!" Tawnia cackled. "Putting on makeup was just an excuse anyway. I'm actually going upstairs to call my mother and tell her we're going to be rich!"

Tawnia grabbed some more popcorn, then thought better of it, and tossed it back before picking up the entire bowl and running up the stairs.

"I'm so, so sorry, honey," Hayley said.

"What for? Oh, you mean strong-arming me into inviting that hideous girl over here for a sleepover just so you could pump her for information?"

"Boy, it really does sound bad when you put it that way."

Gemma grinned. "Don't sweat it. I was happy to do it. I liked Bessie. She was always very sweet to me when she saw me. Constantly offering me some of her candy. I kind of miss her. And if you think there's more to her death than what people are saying, then I say more power to you."

Hayley sat back in her chair, floored by her daughter's sudden mood change. "Who are you? And what have you done with my daughter?"

"I know I've been a little difficult lately—"

"Climbing Mount Everest is difficult. You've been a nightmare."

"Okay, don't make me sound so horrible. It's just . . ."

"What, Gemma?"

Her eyes welled up with tears and she turned away.

Hayley put a comforting arm around her shoulder. "What? You can tell me."

"It's stupid."

"Nothing that upsets you like this is stupid, okay?"

"Next year I'm going to be a senior and then I'm going to graduate. . . ."

"And then you'll go to college. I know."

"All my friends, they already know what they want to do. Carrie Weston is going to go to Boston College and then law school. Kendra's going to be a teacher. Everyone's always asking me, 'What are you going to do?' or 'What do you want to be?' I just draw a blank, because I don't know."

"There's no rush, honey. It's okay not to know."

"But I feel like I'm way behind everybody else."

"Your grades are fine."

"No, I have no idea what I want. And I'm afraid that when the time comes, and all my friends go off to college, I still won't know, and I'll be stuck here forever!"

Gemma sobbed and Hayley hugged her tightly. "It's going to be okay. Trust me. You'll figure it out."

Gemma tried desperately to stop crying. She was a very dramatic kid at times, but she tended to curb her real emotions, keep up a brave front, like nothing bothered her. So this moment had to have been building up inside her for a while now, to the point where she could no longer control it.

"You're a good kid, a smart kid. You impress me every day. I'm not the least bit worried that when the time comes, you'll know which direction to take. And if it doesn't work out, then you go in another direction. Life is one big map. You like visiting some places better than others. But the most important thing to remember is that it's about the journey, not the destination."

"That's a pretty good speech, Mom," Gemma said, wiping her eyes.

"Believe me, I just pulled it out of my butt. This mothering thing didn't come with a manual."

Gemma giggled.

"And, hey, look on the bright side. What's the worst-case scenario? You live with me the rest of your life and we grow old together."

Gemma wailed.

But she was faking it.

Mother and daughter exchanged smirks and then convulsed with laughter.

Hayley hadn't felt this good in a long time.

Island Food & Spirits
by
Hayley Powell

Last night after cooking dinner for the kids, I collapsed in my comfy chair with a glass of wine. (Okay, in the interest of full disclosure, I brought the whole bottle with me; but to be fair, it had been a really stressful day.) I closed my eyes and sipped my wine, grateful for a moment's peace. That's when the phone rang. It was Liddy, who was dying to tell me some new gossip.

My son, Dustin, is an expert at ambushing me when I am at my most vulnerable. Dead tired. Drinking wine. Hearing juicy dirt. How could I possibly focus on anything else? He rattled on about the money he got from his grandmother for Christmas, and how he wanted to spend it on a new video game. There was a big sale at the Bangor Mall on Saturday, and this was his one and only chance to buy the game he wanted. I nodded and waved him away, not really hearing all the details.

So I paid for my lack of concentration the following Saturday in the wee hours of the morning, around seven, when Dustin charged into my bedroom and began shaking me to get up and dressed so we could make the one-hour drive to Bangor before the stores in the mall opened. I simply stared at him. The Bangor Mall on a Saturday? Packed with crowds of obnoxious teenagers and screaming babies? Was he serious?

Apparently he was. "A deal's a deal," he wailed. I knew there was no getting out of it. Note to self: *No more wine after dinner.* I always end up paying for it with days like these.

Dustin invited his best buddy, Spanky, to tag along, which was a godsend. Spanky could keep Dustin company while he picked out his video and then they could hang at the Game Zone while I snuck away to shop for a scarf and sweater to update my work wardrobe.

After arriving at the mall, I told the boys to meet me at the food court in two hours. After some whining and shuffling of the feet, they agreed. Nothing in the stores caught my eye and I got bored pretty quickly. It had only been thirty minutes. I still had another hour and a half before I was scheduled to rendezvous with the boys.

I was thirsty, so I headed over to the food court to buy something to drink. The smell of freshly baked pizza was overpowering. I found myself purchasing a large slice of meat-stuffed pizza, along with my bottle of water. I set my tray down on a table to eat and started people watching.

I began noticing a lot of young couples who had small children in strollers; they were all dressed to the nines in matching colors.

Who has the time to coordinate outfits perfectly like that? They were like Stepford families, and they reminded me of all those popular kids in high school who spent hours on the phone discussing what to wear so they would match and stand out as a clique. I glanced down at my ratty jeans and pink t-shirt that said SAVE THE TA-TA'S, which was a gift from Mona last fall when we participated in the Breast Cancer Walkathon. I felt so uncool.

As I munched on my pizza, I watched some mothers and daughters pass by. The mothers were dressed younger than their kids: miniskirts, thigh-high boots, shiny lip gloss. Gemma would never forgive me if I wore an outfit like that! And they were trashing a friend who wasn't there to defend herself, just laughing and making fun of her. Like overgrown mean girls.

I had to get away from that bad energy. So I got up and walked over to the pretzel cart and purchased a bag of warm salty pretzel nuggets and a cheddar-cheese dipping sauce. A family of five wandered past me. Every single one of them was wearing camouflage hunting jackets and scowls on their faces. They were like those rebellious kids who hate school and spend most of their time congregating outside in the smoking area.

After the salty pretzels, I craved something sweet. I made my way through the crowd to the DQ and ordered a large hot-fudge sundae. That's when it hit me. Shopping at the mall was just like being at high school with all the various cliques, groups of outsiders, popular kids, etc.

"Mom!" Dustin yelled, interrupting my reverie. He and Spanky were staring at me, wide-eyed. "What?" I said. Dustin gestured at the table where I was sitting with a sweep of his arm. I suddenly realized it was littered with pizza crust, two empty water bottles, pretzel crumbs, dollops of cheese dip, crumpled napkins, and a half-eaten ice-cream sundae. Chocolate fudge sauce was dripping down the front of my pink t-shirt. I realized at that moment I was still that same girl in high school too: the one who could always be found sitting in the school cafeteria, eating, people watching, and usually dripping something on her clothes. Some things just never change.

That night my embarrassed son deigned to forgive me, but only because I stopped at the grocery store on the way home and bought the ingredients for homemade hot-fudge sundaes, which I served to him while he played his brand-new video game. I left him to his fun so I could relax with a new, adults-only cocktail I made with the leftover chocolate syrup.

Ultra Alexander

Ingredients

2 ounces brandy
2 ounces crème de cacao
1 tablespoon whipping cream
1 tablespoon chocolate syrup

Fill your cocktail shaker with ice. Add the brandy, crème de cacao, whipping cream, and chocolate syrup. Shake, strain, and serve in a glass.

Hayley's Hot-Fudge Sauce

<u>Ingredients</u>
1½ cups granulated sugar
½ cup brown sugar
¾ cup cocoa
¼ cup all-purpose flour
½ teaspoon salt
1 can evaporated milk (14 ounces)
1 cup water
2 tablespoons butter
2 teaspoons vanilla

Combine the sugar, cocoa, flour, and salt in a saucepan. Add the milk, water, and butter. Cook over medium heat, cool, then stir in the vanilla.

Top over your favorite ice cream and add your favorite toppings.

Chapter 33

Hayley tried to ignore the intoxicating smell of sizzling bacon on the flat grill as she stood behind a hulking brute in a stained white wife-beater shirt and ratty jeans.

"I'm not leaving until you talk to me, Wolf."

Hayley had managed to track down Bessie's loutish ex-boyfriend Wolf Conway at the newly renovated Starfish Diner on Main Street, just a few hundred feet from the town pier.

According to her sources—okay, Mona, who took her entire brood there earlier in the week for their signature eggs Benedict—Wolf was the new cook for the breakfast and lunch shift. Mona was certain it was Wolf because she got into an argument with him over her undercooked side of sausage. They nearly came to blows before the owner, Cindy Callahan, stepped in to defuse the escalating situation by comping Mona's meal.

Cindy was a former Delta Airlines flight attendant

and recent divorcée who took her ex-husband's settlement money and bought the flailing diner. She gave it a much-needed face-lift. She launched her grand opening on the Fourth of July, and quickly drew in a lot of tourists and cruise ship passengers. Now during the bleak winter months, business had slowed considerably, though Cindy was determined to stay open year-round.

When her cook left her high and dry in early February to follow a strapping marine, whom she had met at Drinks Like A Fish, back to his base in warm Florida, Cindy was desperate. Apparently, she knew all about Wolf's run-ins with the law and his unsettling reputation, but the big oaf could fry an egg. Also, as a newly single woman in her late thirties, Cindy appreciated Wolf's muscles, which glistened with sweat from the kitchen heat and flexed so impressively when he used the spatula to flip pancakes.

The restaurant was nearly empty when Hayley arrived, so Cindy was kind enough to allow Hayley to have a word with her employee. Unfortunately, Wolf wasn't nearly as accommodating. With his back to Hayley, he simply chose to ignore her.

"I'm not here to cause you any trouble, Wolf. I just want to talk to you."

Wolf picked up a large knife and began dicing an onion and a green pepper for an omelette.

"There are no customers in the diner, Wolf. I

know you're just making that omelette so you don't have to talk to me."

He kept chopping.

Faster.

Angrier.

"Okay. Would you at least explain why Bessie felt the need to take out a restraining order against you?"

Wolf stopped for a moment.

Gripped the knife more tightly.

Then kept chopping.

He used the knife to scrape the bits of onion and green pepper onto the flat grill. Then he grabbed a tomato and started violently slicing it.

"She told her ex-sister-in-law that she was scared of you and she was afraid of what you might do to her. And now she's dead."

Wolf spun around, brandishing the sharp knife, pointing it at Hayley, who took a step back.

"I didn't do nothing to her. Papers said she died of a heart attack. So, why are you poking your nose where it don't belong?"

Hayley suddenly noticed the distinct T-shaped scar on his left bicep.

Exactly like the one she spotted on the intruder who attacked her at Bessie's house.

It was Wolf Conway.

Wolf noticed Hayley staring at the scar.

His face twitched a little.

He pointed the knife in Hayley's direction.

"Just leave me alone!"

"It was you. You were the one who broke into Bessie's house."

"So you wanna call the cops? Go ahead. Then you can explain what the hell *you* were doing there too!"

"What were you looking for?"

Wolf turned back to the grill, poured some whipped eggs into a small frying pan, along with the veggies and some shredded cheese, and placed it on a red-hot burner, just to the left of the flat grill.

"Talk to me, Wolf. I know it's taken you a long while to find this job. It would be a shame if word got out you were robbing houses."

Wolf twisted back around, waving the knife at Hayley. "Cindy doesn't care about my past. She says she's comfortable with it."

"Yes, but she's probably assuming the past isn't just yesterday when you broke into your ex-girlfriend's house and ransacked it."

"What do you want from me?"

"The truth."

Wolf sighed and lowered the knife, but he still clutched it at his side.

"I wasn't there to steal anything. I just wanted to get back what's mine."

"And what was that?"

"Two grand in cash."

Wolf detected the skepticism on Hayley's face.

"Bessie showed up at my apartment about a week or so before she died. She told me she wanted to get back together."

"I find that hard to believe," Hayley said, folding her arms.

"I did too. She despised me. I couldn't understand what was happening. What suddenly changed her mind? Then I got a phone call while she was there. It was from Cindy. She told me Bessie had been by the diner and told her she should hire me. She said I was a great cook. And Cindy wouldn't regret it. I couldn't believe my ears. Bessie being so nice? It didn't make a lick of sense. But I needed the job. It wasn't until a few days later when I realized why. I knew she was up to no good."

"What?"

"When I took the call from Cindy, I left Bessie alone for a few minutes to give Cindy some information, like my Social Security number, stuff like that for the payroll. When I came back, Bessie couldn't get out of my place fast enough. I didn't care. I was too stoked to be working again. But it was a setup. Bessie knew from when we were together that I always kept about two grand, which my granddaddy left me, in one of his old cigar boxes. I promised him I would never touch it, unless it was an emergency. I kept that promise because he was the only person who was ever nice to me in my whole life. Well, after Cindy hired me, I decided to borrow from the stash to pay my back rent, since I could replace it after I got my first paycheck. Only thing was, when I opened the cigar box, it was empty."

"You think Bessie stole it from you?"

"Damn right, she stole it. She was desperate to start that lousy candy business and she knew I had a hidden stash of cold, hard cash in that cigar box. She convinced Cindy to hire me, probably told her the best time to call me, and made sure she was in my house when the call came in so I would be distracted and she could steal my money and slip out."

"That's what you two were fighting about outside my office that day?"

"She denied taking it, but she was lying. Her face got red when she lied. And that day as she stood in front of me, babbling like a fool that she had no idea what I was talking about, she was flushed redder than this-here ripe tomato."

Wolf slammed the knife down hard, slicing the tomato in half.

Hayley jumped.

Wolf picked up the small frying pan and flipped the omelette over on its other side.

"So that's why you broke into her house? To find your money?"

"She died so soon after that, I figured there was a chance she didn't spend all of it yet, so I decided to see if I could at least get some of it back."

Wolf was violent and troubled and desperate.

But in Hayley's gut, she felt he wasn't a killer.

"Hayley, are you putting the moves on my manly cook?" Cindy Callahan cooed as she sashayed into the kitchen. She was dressed in a bright baby blue sweater, white pearls, and jean skirt. She was freshly made-up, and her dark brown hair was teased out.

"Uh, no, Cindy. We're just talking. Right, Wolf?"

Wolf nodded, eyeing Cindy, well, wolfishly.

Cindy walked past Hayley and rubbed Wolf's left bicep with the scar on it.

"You feel this, Hayley?" Cindy asked.

"Looks pretty impressive, I'd say," Hayley said, trying to be polite.

"You could crack a walnut on it. And believe me, I have," Cindy said, laughing. "Now, if you're done harassing my big boy here, a family of four just came in and they want my world-famous blueberry waffles."

Hayley eyed Wolf.

He smiled lovingly at Cindy before turning his eyes back toward Hayley.

"Nice talking to you, Hayley."

Hayley nodded and turned to walk out.

She heard slobbering kissing behind her.

Wolf was well on his way to securing his very own sugar mommy.

Chapter 34

Hayley was certain she was about to be fired.

When she returned to the office after confronting Wolf Conway at the Starfish Diner, Sal met her at the door, commented on how her lunch hour was more like a lunch hour and a half, and then ordered her to follow him to his office.

Hayley's stomach did flip-flops as she bowed her head, chastised, and hoped she would be eligible for unemployment benefits once she was kicked to the curb.

In hindsight maybe zealously pursuing this "Bessie Winthrop was murdered" theory might have been a massive mistake.

Sal ushered her inside and told her to take a seat.

Hayley sat down.

Sal slammed the door shut. He crossed behind her and plopped down at his desk and stared coldly at her.

Hayley sat straight up, her mind racing to come up with two or three arguments for why she should not be terminated.

Her mind was blank.

There had to be one.

Think, Hayley, think.

"You've sure got a lot of spunk," Sal barked.

Hayley nodded. This was just like the pilot episode of *The Mary Tyler Moore Show*, a classic sitcom from the 1970s that Hayley had watched in reruns on TV Land. The irascible newsroom producer, Lou Grant, said the same thing to Mary Richards in her job interview to work at the station as an associate producer. Mary beamed proudly and said, "Well, yes . . ." before Mr. Grant cut her off and yelled, "I *hate* spunk!"

She waited for Sal to tell her off.

Mary did wind up getting the job in that classic pilot episode.

But Hayley wasn't so confident that she was going to walk out of here with her job intact.

Sal just stared at her, not cracking a smile.

Hayley shifted uncomfortably in her chair.

Sal finally spoke. "I guess congratulations are in order."

"Congratulations? For what?"

"I just got off the phone with Sabrina Merry-weather."

"Uh-oh. What did she say?"

"She spent most of the conversation trashing you with a lot of four-letter words. I served in the army back in the day, when I had hair on my head and about a hundred less pounds hanging over my belt, and I swear I never heard such foul language. She really has it out for you."

"Well, we never were the best of friends, to be honest."

"And I don't think at this point you ever will be. Those columns about Bessie Winthrop you've been writing finally did the trick. The mayor's office has been inundated with calls demanding she have the coroner exhume Bessie's body for a more thorough autopsy than just the preliminary one Sabrina performed last week. And for some strange reason, and I don't even want to know why, the mayor seems to be scared of you and what you've been writing, so she pressured Dr. Merryweather to do just that, hoping they could finally put the whole matter to rest."

"When is she going to conduct the second autopsy?"

"Already done."

"And?" Hayley said, holding her breath.

"Upon closer inspection, Dr. Merryweather found large amounts of some medication called Mephyton in Bessie's system."

"Mephyton? What's that?"

"A concentrated form of vitamin K used to treat hemophiliacs, people with vitamin K deficiencies. It's a natural blood thickener used to promote clotting."

"But Bessie had heart disease. A blood clot to her arteries could kill her."

"Exactly."

"Are you saying—"

"Dr. Merryweather spoke to Bessie's doctor. Ever since her last physical, he was worried about her heart and was after her to start taking War-farin, which is an anticoagulant that helps prevent harmful clots from forming in the blood vessels. He phoned a prescription into the pharmacy, and Bessie promised to pick it up and finally start the regimen."

"Well, if she was supposed to be on a blood thinner, then how the hell did she wind up taking a blood *thickener*?"

"Beats me. Unless someone switched the medications. Chief Alvares talked to the pharmacy and Bessie did stop by a few weeks before she died to pick up her prescription."

"So whoever switched the medications had to have been close to Bessie. Someone she would have allowed inside her house."

"Or someone could have broken into her house while she wasn't there and did the switch."

Someone like Wolf Conway?

"So Bessie basically killed herself without realizing it."

"With someone's help. We just don't know who yet."

Finally her suspicions were being confirmed.

And it would have felt gratifying if Hayley didn't feel so sad that Bessie was gone.

Hayley suddenly perked up. "So, does this mean . . . ?"

Sal nodded. "Chief Alvares has already reclassified Bessie's death as a homicide."

Victory!

Chapter 35

As she left the office at five-thirty that afternoon, Hayley was grateful she still had her job. Normally, quitting time was five o'clock, but Sal was determined she make up for the extra half hour she took at lunch to question Wolf Conway at the Starfish Diner.

Wolf Conway. Could it have been him?

He wasn't exactly a brain trust.

Switching Bessie's medication would require knowing a blood thickener from a blood thinner.

And Hayley was guessing he could barely read a children's book, let alone a doctor's prescription.

Besides, he was more focused on retrieving the money Bessie had stolen from him than Bessie herself.

If he had killed Bessie, it would more likely have been in the moment—a crime of passion, not a carefully thought-out murder plot.

Clearly, thinking wasn't his strong suit.

Then who?
Ron Hopkins?
Cody Donovan?
Cody's gun-toting, soon-to-be ex-wife, Kerry?
Mark and Mary Garber?
Mayor Richards?

None of them needed alibis because Bessie's death happened over the course of a few weeks. All of them could have somehow switched the medications at any time.

It would be impossible, even with the most painstakingly detailed timeline, to determine how and when the killer gained access to Bessie's house to swap out the meds.

Hayley's phone buzzed.

A text from Liddy: **At Drinks Like A Fish. Need you here. Now.**

Shockingly, Hayley was in no mood for cocktails at her brother's bar. She just wanted to go home and check on Gemma and Dustin.

But Liddy's text sounded urgent enough for her to swing by on her way, just to make sure her friend was okay.

The bar was full when she arrived a few minutes later.

After a long day at the store, four cashiers from the Shop 'n Save were unwinding with Cosmos at a corner table.

Liddy sat atop her usual stool, near the front of the bar, sipping a mojito.

Hayley joined her. "Hey, what's up?"

"I may have something for you. Let me order you a drink first. What are you having?"

"No, thanks. Not in a drinking mood."

Liddy nearly fell off her stool, before catching herself. She stared at Hayley, a stunned look on her face. "I'm sorry. I thought I heard you say . . ."

Hayley waved at the bartender, who strolled out through the kitchen doors. "Club soda with lime, please, Michelle."

Michelle stopped in her tracks and giggled. "Somebody turn down the jukebox. I didn't hear you. I thought you said—"

"I'm not drinking tonight."

Except for a Bruno Mars song playing softly on the jukebox, the whole bar fell silent.

"Seriously, I can't take a night off?" Hayley scoffed, annoyed by the dramatic reaction to her one night on the wagon.

Michelle filled a glass with club soda, squeezed a lime over the ice, and delivered it to Hayley. "Everything okay, sweetie?"

"Yes. Thank you, Michelle," Hayley said before turning to the table of cashiers. "Nothing's wrong, ladies. Is it so hard to believe I'm taking one night off from alcohol?"

The cashiers shook their heads in unison, but it was obvious they weren't giving Hayley an honest answer.

"Look, I can't stay," Hayley said to Liddy. "What's

so important you couldn't have told me over the phone?"

"Sonny and I had sex in the shower this morning."

"Wow. Now that's a visual I'm not going to shake for a while. But thanks for sharing."

"That's not the important part. Well, for me it is. You wouldn't believe how hot and erotic it was. I felt like Angie Dickinson in that scene from *Dressed to Kill*, when that muscle-bound, naked man came up behind her through the steam in the shower as she was soaping herself down, and then she woke up and it was a dream. Only, mine wasn't a dream, and——"

"Liddy, please!"

"Okay, well, when we were done and drying each other off——"

"I don't need every detail!"

"Okay, well, like I told you, Sonny loves pillow talk. Except we weren't in bed with our heads on the pillow. Like I said, we were in the shower——"

"Liddy!"

"Right. Sorry. Stay with me. You're going to like this. Sonny's been really busy lately, and he's been behind in his work, mostly because he's been preoccupied finding my erogenous zones. . . ."

Hayley opened her mouth to protest, but Liddy held up a hand to stop her.

"I know, I know. Too much information. Well,

he finally started processing the paperwork for Bessie's estate. Well, what little of it there is. . . . Just a few measly dollars, and most of it will go to the new owners of her cats for the feeding and care of the pets. But there was a life insurance policy—"

"Yes, I know. The money is going to Bessie's niece, Tawnia."

"No, it's not."

"What do you mean?"

"Bessie had Sonny revise the policy right before she died. . . ."

"Who?"

"Her daughter."

Even Bruno Mars crooning from the jukebox wasn't loud enough to drown out Liddy. The cashiers at the corner table sprang to attention at the mention of a daughter.

"But Bessie didn't have a daughter . . . ," Hayley said.

"Sonny claims she did, and Bessie insisted on changing the name of the beneficiary from her deadbeat brother's kid to her own daughter."

"A daughter? But how? What's her name?"

"Well, that I don't know, because, I guess, I seemed a little too interested. Sonny suddenly had a crisis of conscience then and started prattling on about professional ethics and how he had already said too much. He just shut down on me. Believe me, I tried a lot of X-rated tricks to get him to open up, and, well, you know how persuasive I can be when I put my mind to it—"

"No, I don't! And I don't want to know!"

"No matter what I did, I just couldn't get him to crack. He moaned so loud that I thought my neighbors were going to call the police, but I still couldn't break him."

"I don't get it. Why would Bessie hide the fact that she had a daughter? And when? I've known her since high school and I've never seen her pregnant."

"What are you talking about? She constantly looked pregnant . . . ," Liddy said before catching herself. "Sorry. That came out wrong."

One of the cashiers at the corner table, Hannah O'Bannon, a towering woman, with stringy brown hair and glasses, who rang up Hayley's order the day she won the grand prize on *Wild and Crazy Couponing*, a game show that shot an episode in Bar Harbor recently, turned her head toward Hayley. "There were rumors. . . ."

"Rumors? What rumors?"

"Bessie was in my class in high school. She left junior year to go to ballet school in New York City, or at least that's the story she told, but nobody believed her. I mean, seriously, Bessie a ballerina?"

"You think she got pregnant and used ballet as an excuse to get out of town?"

"We know she had an aunt in Toronto and she'd go visit her sometimes. That's where everybody assumed she went."

"If she was pregnant, then who was the father?"

"There was a lot of speculation. A lot of us believed it was Mr. Draper."

"The biology teacher?"

"Yes. Biology! You would think he would have known better!" Hannah said. "Anyway, Bessie was always getting A's in his class, and she didn't know the first thing about the human body or dissecting a frog. I was her lab partner and I constantly had to cover her ass. But she was Mr. Draper's little pet and could do no wrong, and she was always staying after school to ask him questions about our homework assignments and she would be in there forever. We'd see her sneaking out of his classroom after we got done with cheerleading practice and it would be close to five o'clock. I mean, really, what were they doing in there all that time?"

"Wow. Mr. Draper," Hayley said.

"Well, this is just outrageous!" Liddy screamed.

"It happens, Liddy. Teachers sleep with students. It's not right, but it happens."

"I know it happens! I just find it outrageous that he would sleep with Bessie Winthrop and not make one move on *me*! I was so much prettier than Bessie! Why didn't he pick me to hit on? It makes absolutely no sense!"

"Okay, missing the point, Liddy. Let's try to stay on topic. So if the rumors are true, and Bessie gave birth to a baby during junior year and then gave her up for adoption, then she'd have to be at least eighteen or nineteen by now. Maybe there was some kind of a clause that said when the daughter legally became an adult, she could see the adoption papers and track down her birth mother."

"So you think they reconnected and began a relationship?" Hannah asked as all the women at the corner table leaned in, engrossed in the conversation.

"I'd put money on it, even though I don't have any," Hayley said. "And if Bessie grew fond of her, that would explain why she made the change to her life insurance policy. She probably wanted to make sure her biological daughter was taken care of. Her generosity would go a long way to relieve the guilt she probably felt for giving her up when she was born."

Given this new information, the most likely scenario would be Tawnia finding out that Bessie intended to erase her name from the life insurance policy, and then deciding to knock her aunt off before she had a chance to do it. But if that was the case, she'd have to get rid of her immediately, and the bad effects of the blood-thickening drugs took weeks to take their toll on Bessie's heart. Tawnia also claimed she and her mother had no idea there even was a life insurance policy. She could have been lying, but Hayley doubted it.

Her best bet in finding out the truth was Jimmy MacDonald.

The pharmacist.

Maybe the rash of recent pharmacy thefts weren't the sole work of some local hooligans trying to get a quick fix with OxyContin.

Maybe one of those thefts included a big bottle of Mephyton tablets.

The same ones that clogged poor Bessie Winthrop's heart and killed her.

Chapter 36

Jimmy MacDonald scratched the back of his head as he scrolled down a list of medications. "Nope. None of the meds that were stolen were Mephyton, Hayley. Just OxyContin."

"The only way anyone could have gotten his or her hands on it would have to have been through a pharmacy. Which means if it wasn't stolen, then it was prescribed to someone with either a vitamin K deficiency or hemophilia or some other condition that would require a coagulant," Hayley said.

"Sorry, Hayley. I'm already taking a risk telling you what meds were missing. Disclosing patient information is not only a fireable offense, I'd probably be breaking a few laws too, and I'm too close to retirement to lose my pension now and spend my twilight years behind bars."

"I understand, Jimmy. I would never ask you to do anything that could get you into trouble."

"I appreciate you understanding," Jimmy said,

eyeing the plump blond woman in a blue apron vest who was positioned up the aisle in the front of the store. "Looks like Deanna at the register is ready for her break. She usually takes a good fifteen minutes walking down the street to the Big Apple for a coffee."

Hayley nodded, not quite sure why this information was relevant.

Jimmy removed his lab coat and laid it down on the pharmacy counter. "I usually close up shop here for a bit and cover for her. That's where I'll be. Waiting on any customers, who might come into the store. But right now, the store is pretty empty, so there shouldn't be anyone wandering around back here. You'll be all alone. Just saying."

Jimmy gave her a conspiratorial wink and wandered up the aisle, taking his place behind the cash register as Deanna threw on her winter coat and exited out the sliding glass doors.

Once she was gone, Jimmy called out to Hayley, "Guess I'll take this opportunity to restock the mints and gum over at the last register, where I can't see anything that's going on back there!"

Hayley took her cue and bounded behind the counter lickety-split. She kept one eye on the front door to make sure no one strolled in and spotted her as she threw on Jimmy's lab coat. She figured if anyone did catch her scrolling through the pharmacy records on Jimmy's computer, she could claim she was working a part-time job as a pharmacy assistant to pay her astronomical winter heating bill. The whole town knew how cheap Sal was, so it was more than likely most people would totally buy it.

Hayley quickly typed *Mephyton* into the search engine and hit the return button. The computer was agonizingly slow.

She heard Jimmy whistling an old Glen Campbell song "Wichita Lineman" as he ripped open a carton of Tic Tacs and started unpacking them.

"Come on, come on . . . ," Hayley whispered to herself as the computer continued to load a page.

Finally a list of names appeared under the heading of Mephyton.

Four in all.

Three names she didn't recognize.

Probably summer residents who were long gone.

The dates of their last prescription refills were in August and September.

Only one name was issued a Mephyton prescription more recently.

In January.

Right about the time Bessie started taking the anticoagulant medication for her heart.

Marla Heasley.

Dr. Palmer's plucky, cat-loving, devoted, and fiercely jealous assistant.

Chapter 37

Hayley tried calling Sergio, but she got his voice mail.

This was explosive information about Dr. Palmer's assistant, Marla Heasley.

The pieces of the puzzle were finally coming together.

It was late Friday afternoon, and Hayley hoped Aaron was still at the office so she could quietly sit him down and explain, out of earshot, her suspicions about Marla. She was certain he would have enough information on Marla's identity on file to confirm her theory. Then she could turn everything over to Sergio, and he could take it from there.

However, when she arrived at the vet's office and parked her car, she noticed Dr. Palmer's parking space was empty.

She casually strolled inside to find Marla seated

at the reception desk in her bright pink scrubs emblazoned with Archie comic-book characters. She was flipping through the latest issue of *In Touch* magazine, engrossed in all the latest gossip about all her favorite Hollywood stars' most recent exploits.

Marla looked up at Hayley and grimaced, irritated she had to deal with her once again.

"Here to ransack the office?" Marla said, sneering.

"No. I'd like to have a word with Aaron. Do you know when he'll be back?"

"What do you want to talk to him about?"

"It's a private matter."

"Well, the doctor is a very busy man."

"I'm sure he's going to want to hear this."

"Look, when it comes to crackpot stalkers, I'm Dr. Palmer's first line of defense. So if you want to talk to him, you have to go through me."

"'Crackpot stalker'? Seriously?"

"He caught you looting his office! What else do you want to call it?"

She had to admit the girl had a point.

Hayley's eyes fell on a small white bottle on Marla's desk, next to the stack of glossy magazines.

"What are you looking at?" Marla hissed.

"Nothing," Hayley said, quickly averting her eyes.

"You trying to get a look at my meds? Mind your own business," Marla said, snatching up the bottle and stuffing it into her bag on the floor. "Since you're so curious, I have a vitamin K deficiency. Nothing serious. It's nothing you can use to get me fired."

"I'm not trying to get you fired, Marla."

"Yes, you are. Ever since you first showed up here and set your sights on Dr. Palmer, you've had it out for me. You feel threatened by me. Well, don't worry. I'll be leaving town soon, so I'll finally be out of your hair and you can have him all to yourself."

"Marla, I'm not trying to get between you and the doctor, or get you fired. I don't care about your future plans and that you take Mephyton. I just want to speak to Dr. Palmer. So, where can I find him?"

Marla's face went pale. "How did you know I was taking Mephyton?"

Hayley kicked herself.

Stupid, stupid, stupid.

"I saw the label on the bottle."

"From way over there? You must have X-ray vision."

"I had LASIK surgery a few years back. I have better than twenty-twenty vision."

"I'd say. The label was turned toward me. You would have had to see through the plastic bottle."

"Or maybe I read about it on the Internet—"

"You just happened to be researching vitamin K deficiencies on the Internet? Now that's a remarkable coincidence."

Hayley knew she had blown it.

Her best course of action was just to leave now.

She grabbed her phone out of the back pocket of her jeans. "Forget it, Marla. I'm just going to call him. That's right. I have his personal cell phone number from when we went out on a date."

"Yeah, I heard how well that turned out."

"Good-bye, Marla," Hayley said, pivoting to leave.

"Wait. He's in his office."

"But his car is gone."

"It broke down on his way in this morning. I had to pick him up at the garage and drive him to work."

"Are you lying to me?"

"Go see for yourself."

With her phone still in her hand, Hayley marched past Marla toward Aaron's office.

The door was open a crack and the light was on inside.

She knocked on the door. "Aaron, can I come in?"

Suddenly she was violently shoved from behind. She pitched forward, dropping her cell phone, her hands outstretched to break her fall as she crashed to the floor.

Her cell phone clattered next to her; but before she could react, Marla scooped it up and slammed the door shut, locking it from outside.

Hayley looked around.

Her first instincts were right.

Marla was indeed lying.

There was no sign of Dr. Palmer.

Hayley sprang to her feet, first trying the knob and then banging hard on the door. "Marla, this is crazy! Open up! You can't keep me prisoner in here! Marla!"

Nothing.

Just a few dogs were barking in their cages, excited by Hayley's loud pounding.

"Marla, it's no use. I know the truth, and it's only a matter of time before the police do too. I've already put a call in to them. Marla?"

Still, nothing.

Hayley dashed over to the phone on Dr. Palmer's desk and picked up the receiver.

The line was dead.

Marla must have unplugged the system from outside.

There was no window in the office to climb out.

She was trapped.

She ran back to the door.

Pounded several more times.

Then she rested her head against it; her mind was racing to come up with some means of escape.

After what seemed like an eternity, she heard a mousy voice coming from the other side of the door. "So, what do you think you know?"

Hayley took a deep breath. "I know you were

adopted, and I know Bessie Winthrop was your biological mother. I know when you turned eighteen, you were able to look at the records and get in touch with her. Which is why you moved here and got a job as Dr. Palmer's assistant. Knowing Bessie as I do, I figure she was feeling lonely and was more than happy to reconnect with the daughter she had given up when Bessie was in high school."

Hayley paused, then pressed her ear to the door. "Marla?"

"Go on," she heard Marla say quietly.

"You worked hard to make a good impression on Bessie, and to worm your way into her heart, to the point where Bessie wanted to make up for not being there for you all those years. She must have told you she was making you the beneficiary of a very generous life insurance policy. That was your ticket out of Maine—your way to Hollywood so you could finally live the life of all those glamorous celebrities you constantly were reading about and worshiping so much."

Hayley heard sniffling coming from the other side of the door.

"I just want to be like my idol, Selena Gomez. Have my own TV show, do movies, maybe get a recording contract."

"And Bessie dying was your only chance to get your hands on the capital you would need to make your dreams come true."

"She was already sick. Everyone said she was

a walking time bomb. I was just speeding up the inevitable."

"You did your research and realized your own meds would go a long way in accelerating poor Bessie's demise. So you swapped out her meds with yours and just waited. Bessie was taking fist-fuls a day, believing they were thinning her blood. In reality they were causing deadly clots, which left unchecked would surely kill her. And they did. When you read that the coroner wasn't going to perform an autopsy, and Bessie's death was deter-mined to be from natural causes, you thought you were in the clear. You were just sticking around long enough to pocket your money and then you were going to blow town."

"I told Bessie I wanted to be a famous actress and move to Hollywood, and she was very sup-portive. She said she would help me in any way she could."

"I'm not sure she understood exactly *how much* it was going to cost her."

"I liked Bessie. I know what I did was wrong, but at least she never had a clue what I was up to. I take comfort in that."

"You shouldn't. The reason you're never going to be a star is because you're a lousy actress."

"No, I'm not!"

"You may have *acted* fond of Bessie, but she sus-pected you were up to something. She just didn't know what it was or how you were going to do it. But as her health worsened from those counter-productive meds, she took out another small insurance policy, just in case."

"What do you mean?"

"She put a little note inside some candy she made especially for me. In case something happened to her. She knew how dogged I can be when I think something's fishy. So Bessie insured I wouldn't let the real facts be brushed underneath the carpet. And her note did just the trick. And here we are."

Hayley listened for a moment.

There was silence on the other side of the door.

"Marla? Marla, where did you go? Are you still out there?"

Nothing.

Hayley banged on the door again.

"Marla?"

Five minutes passed.

Hayley sat on the floor, knees to her chest, rocking back and forth, trying to figure out how she was ever going to get out of this one.

The kids would know something was wrong if she didn't come home.

Then they would call Sergio.

He would retrace her steps to the pharmacy, and Jimmy MacDonald would show him the records Hayley had been scrolling through.

Sergio would see Marla Heasley's name. Hopefully, that would be enough to get him to drive over to Dr. Palmer's office, looking for her.

And he would burst through the door and rescue Hayley.

Yes, that was what was going to happen.

Positive thoughts.

Positive thoughts.

It was still quiet outside the office door.

The dogs in their cages had calmed down and stopped barking.

Hayley thought Marla had left, because Marla's best bet at this point was keeping Hayley locked up while she got a head start out of town. By the time she was discovered, Marla would be long gone and on the run. But the state troopers would be alerted and an all-out manhunt dispatched; with any luck Marla would be captured before crossing state lines.

There was a *click.*

Someone was outside unlocking the door.

Hayley jumped to her feet.

The door slowly swung open.

Hayley was dead wrong.

Marla hadn't fled the scene at all.

She was standing in the doorway. There was a wild look on her face as she brandished a large syringe.

Chapter 38

"What is that?" Hayley asked, backing away.

"Pentobarbital or sodium thiopental. It's what we use to euthanize the poor sick animals we just can't save—"

"Sodium what?"

"It doesn't matter. All you need to know is it causes unconsciousness, followed by respiratory and then cardiac arrest."

Hayley put up her hand, pleading. "Marla, please don't do anything you're going to regret—"

"If there is one thing I know I won't regret, it's shutting you up for good!" Marla said, raising the syringe like a knife, inching toward Hayley.

"Now I know why Blueberry liked you so much. Evil attracts evil!"

Marla let out a ghastly scream, like a war cry, and charged Hayley.

Hayley threw her arms up as Marla plunged the

syringe toward her chest. Hayley locked her hands around Marla's wrist.

The two women struggled over possession of the syringe.

Marla kicked Hayley's shins with her feet and clawed at her face with her free hand.

Hayley kept her eyes locked on the needle while grappling for it as it swung away from her chest and over her face, settling above her left eye.

If she gave even an inch, the needle would plunge directly into her iris.

Marla backed Hayley up against Dr. Palmer's desk, forcing Hayley up on top of it as folders, pens, letter openers, and framed photographs were swept off by the fierce struggle.

Down the hall, from their cages, agitated dogs barked and frightened cats meowed.

Marla was younger and stronger and used that to her advantage in order to pin Hayley down on the desk, forcing an arm down over her neck while trying to inject her with the syringe. However, Hayley still had a mighty grip on Marla's wrist, making it difficult to finish her off.

But Hayley felt her grip weakening.

Marla was getting the best of her.

She couldn't believe it was going to end like this.

Euthanized like a decrepit, old dog in a vet's office.

Her arm was ready to give out.

Marla managed to lower the needle so it was now just two inches from Hayley's right cheek.

Suddenly a booming voice startled both of them. "What the hell is going on here?"

Marla twisted her head around.

A shocked Dr. Palmer stood in the doorway in a brown leather winter coat and a tan scarf around his neck.

Hayley seized the opportunity to bring her knee up and drive it into Marla's stomach.

She felt a gush of hot air on her face as it got knocked out of Marla.

Hayley wrenched Marla's hand gripping the syringe away from her.

The needle grazed Marla's upper left arm.

Everyone froze in place.

Marla stared at her arm and watched in horror as a small line of blood began staining her pink Archie scrubs from the inside.

"Oh, my God! Oh, my God!" Marla wailed, sinking to the floor, in shock. "I don't want to die! I don't want to die!"

Hayley bolted out of the office past a still-stunned Dr. Palmer. She spotted her cell phone lying on the floor, where Marla had tossed it. She grabbed it. The screen was cracked, but the phone was still working.

Hayley punched in 9-1-1.

Once the paramedics were on their way, Hayley finally relaxed.

She knew Marla would survive.

It was just a surface scratch.

There wouldn't be enough of the drugs in her system to cause any serious damage.

Hayley was dazed and exhausted.

She didn't even have enough energy to react when Dr. Palmer took her in his arms, hugging and comforting her.

Still, she knew it felt good.

Chapter 39

The following Monday, Hayley's final column on the Bessie Winthrop murder was printed in the *Island Times*. Sal gruffly apologized for not believing in her previously hidden investigative-reporting talents. He didn't want to make a big deal about Hayley being right. However, with the flood of congratulatory phone calls from locals impressed with how Hayley blew the case wide open, he was left with little choice.

Sergio held a press conference with a few of the local broadcast networks praising Hayley's dogged pursuit of justice, and both Gemma and Dustin were excited to hear their mother's name mentioned on the news.

There was silence from the coroner's office. After being deluged over the weekend with calls from all over the state demanding to know how she could so publicly botch a case, Sabrina issued a curt statement from her office that announced she had "been called out of town for a family emergency and would address all questions" upon her return.

Probably in about a month when all the brouhaha died down. Hayley was guessing Sabrina was licking her wounds at an exclusive spa that Hayley could never afford.

As infuriated as Sabrina probably still was at Hayley, it didn't even compare to Bruce Linney's reaction when he returned from his Mexican vacation, only to discover his crime beat column had been hijacked by a crusading do-gooder who insisted on embarrassing all of his sources at the police station and county coroner's office.

He accused Hayley of trumpeting her own brother-in-law's incompetence as chief of police.

Hayley quietly informed him that Sergio had personally called her to thank her for keeping his department on their toes, and that he was not the bitter and resentful type. He was more interested in carrying out justice.

Bruce, however, was the bitter and resentful type. It was clear he was just lashing out, enraged that Hayley was a local hero simply by filling in for him while he was gone.

Sal had to assure Bruce his job was safe, and Hayley was going to stick to her food-and-cocktails columns, but that did little to alleviate the tension in the office all morning.

Finally, unable to take it anymore, Sal marched

out of his office. "Hayley, take the rest of the day off. You deserve it."

"But I'm swamped with work, Sal. Look at my in-box."

"I don't care. It'll keep until tomorrow. Hopefully, by then, Bruce will be over his little tantrum, and things can get back to normal around here."

Hayley wasn't about to argue.

She knew exactly what she was going to do with her free day.

She drove straight to the high school and signed out Gemma from study hall so she could take her to lunch.

When Gemma was called to the office and saw her mother standing there, waiting for her, she was more than a little concerned. "Oh, God, whatever you think I did, I'm innocent."

"I don't think you did anything."

"Then why are you here? Oh no, did someone else die?"

"No one died. We're going to lunch."

"Seriously? You want me to play hookey with you?"

"I got a copy of your schedule. You only have two study halls and a gym class for the rest of the day, and you can do your math and history homework assignments after supper tonight. Come on, let's go."

Gemma was still hesitant, but she obediently followed her mother to the car. She kept glancing at Hayley during the ride back to town, waiting for the other shoe to drop. But it never did, and before long they were seated in a booth at Geddy's restaurant, sharing a plate of fried clams, and looking out at the cold gray ocean surrounding the nearly empty town pier.

"All the kids at school were talking about what a hero you are for fighting off that crazy girl who tried to kill you. Everybody's calling me 'Wonder Girl' and my mom 'Wonder Woman.'"

"You must hate that."

"No. It's kind of cool," Gemma said, dunking a clam into a small plastic cup of tartar sauce and popping it into her mouth.

"Gemma, I want to talk to you—"

"I knew it. Here it comes. . . ."

"No. I know it's been tough for you lately, and you're struggling to find your place in the world—"

"Mom . . ."

"Hear me out. You will figure everything out—"

"Mom, it's okay. I'm not depressed anymore. In fact, I've already figured it out."

"What?"

"What I want to do. I got to thinking about it that night Leroy ate those chocolates and we rushed him over to Dr. Palmer's office. I felt so scared and I wanted to help him so bad, but I didn't know what to do. I felt so helpless. I adore animals so much, and I love taking care of them—"

"Well, there was that hamster I bought for you that you forgot to feed and—"

"I was seven! I've grown up since then. And now I'm pretty sure I want to be a vet."

A vet.

Hayley's heart burst with pride.

It was so obvious and perfect, and she couldn't believe she hadn't thought of it before.

She wanted to reach out and grab her daughter and squeeze her like a big mama bear hugging one of her cubs.

But the look on Gemma's face was very clear. She did not want her mother gushing or making a scene or displaying any emotion or shows of affection.

Hayley did her best to keep herself composed.

But, damn, it was hard.

Hayley took a deep breath, kept her cool, and nodded. "I think that's a fine plan."

The best thing she could have done was to act nonchalant and change the subject.

But rarely did Hayley Powell make the best choices.

She just couldn't help herself.

"Remember, veterinarian schools are next to impossible to get into. So if you're serious, you're going to have keep those grades up—"

"Mother!"

"Okay, you're right. I'm done talking."

"As if that's a promise you have any hope of keeping."

Such sarcasm.

Where does she get that from?

After lunch Hayley drove Gemma home. When they walked into the house, Hayley stopped suddenly.

"Do you hear that?"

"Hear what?"

"Exactly. It's quiet. Where are the pets?"

They walked into the living room. Leroy and Blueberry were curled up next to each other on the couch, sleeping soundly. Leroy was snoring gently. Blueberry was purring softly.

"Looks like they've called a truce," Gemma said.

"For now. They can't be at each other's throats twenty-four/seven."

"I think you should give him a chance."

"Blueberry? I don't know, Gemma. He's got a pretty nasty disposition."

"I'm not talking about the cat. That matter is settled. Look at him. He's not going anywhere. We're stuck with him."

"I know. I just wasn't ready to face it."

"I'm talking about Dr. Palmer."

"Oh, Gemma, please . . ."

"You like him. And he likes you."

"It's not a matter of me giving him a chance. We already tried going out and it was a disaster."

"But that was before you exposed his assistant

as a killer. You practically saved his life. He has to be grateful for that."

"I'm not sure I want to date a man because he feels grateful."

"Just call him. Invite him over for dinner."

"I'm sorry, sweetheart. That ship has sailed. I'm not going to embarrass myself any further."

Chapter 40

Gemma wanted to scream, but she was so excited that only a tiny squeak managed to escape her mouth. She waved her arms and appeared to be hyperventilating.

Hayley took a step forward to make sure she could catch her in the event she passed out.

"Thank you! Thank you! Thank you!" Gemma gasped.

"You're doing *me* the favor. I could sure use the help," Dr. Aaron Palmer said as he sat at the dining-room table while Hayley refilled his wine-glass. "As you and everybody else in town knows by now, I have an opening."

Hayley had lasted maybe twelve hours before Gemma put the pressure on her again and forced her to call Dr. Palmer. After stammering on the phone about how sorry she was that his assistant had been arrested and charged with first-degree murder, and how it was all her fault that he found himself now short of help, the conversation managed to wind its way around to a casual dinner invite—nothing special, just trying a new chicken mole recipe.

To her utter shock, Aaron happily accepted, and now it was the following Friday evening. Dustin had escaped to his friend Spanky's house; Gemma was going to go out to the movies with some girlfriends; Aaron was in her house, looking relaxed and gorgeous, his light blue dress shirt open just enough to show off a muscular, bronzed chest.

Who has a bronzed chest in Maine during winter?

The man was practically a god.

But the biggest surprise was when Gemma stopped by the dining-room table to say hello on her way out. After a brief discussion about her veterinarian goals and asking his advice on schools, Aaron offered her a part-time job in his office answering phones and scheduling appointments after school.

Gemma was elated.

It was a giant step forward.

Actual on-the-job training.

Hayley couldn't believe it herself.

If she wasn't fond of Aaron before, watching her daughter's eyes light up, hearing the excitement in her voice, imagining the possibilities racing through her mind, well, for him to do all that, she was more than fond of him now.

A horn honked outside.

"I have to go. The movie starts in ten minutes and I hate missing the previews."

"I'm the same way," Aaron said, laughing. "When do you want me to start?"

"How about Monday?"

Gemma nodded, thanked him again, and floated out the door.

Hayley set the bottle of wine down on the table.

Aaron reached out just as she let go of the bottle and took her hand.

She stood there, not quite sure what to do or how to react. Should she say something?

He just sat in the dining-room chair, holding her hand, smiling up at her.

Then he took the napkin out of his lap and placed it on the table. He stood up to face Hayley.

Her heart was beating so loud that she was sure Leroy and Blueberry could hear it from the other room.

"I know things between us got off to a messy start," Aaron said, slipping an arm around her waist and pulling her toward him. "But you know what? Sometimes I like messy."

He kissed her.

Softly.

The scent of a strong, manly cologne wafted up her nostrils.

Her knees were weak.

His hand was now cradling the back of her head as he pulled her even closer, until the tips of their noses were touching.

Their lips locked.

Hayley tried desperately not to swoon.

She would hate to be considered a swooner.

Too late.

Hayley swooned.

Finally, after a long, intoxicating, passionate kiss, they slowly pulled apart.

And stared at each other.

Smiling.

The silence was too much for her. "We haven't even gotten to the main course. I thought the way to a man's heart was through his stomach. All you've had so far is a salad."

Aaron laughed.

The romantic moment was abruptly interrupted by a loud knock at the front door.

"I don't know who that could be. I'll be right back."

Aaron nodded, then sat back down at the table and took a sip of his wine.

Hayley crossed out of the dining room, through the living room to the front porch, and opened the door.

"Surprise," a man's voice said.

Hayley stood there numbly.

At first, she thought her eyes were playing tricks on her.

It couldn't be.

Whatever they had was over.

He left town.

Never to return.

But here he was.

Right now.

In this moment.

Standing before her, with flowers in one hand and a box of chocolates in the other.

"I know I'm a little late, but Happy Valentine's Day."

Lex Bansfield was back.

Island Food & Spirits
by
Hayley Powell

As many of you know by now, yesterday there was a lovely memorial service for the late Bessie Winthrop, and I was very pleased to see it so well attended. This is one of the nice things about our town. When one of us departs, there is usually a good send-off.

However, I was a little surprised to notice not as many people attended the reception immediately following the service, which usually is the high point of any Bar Harbor funeral. There is always lots of food and fond memories. I think that may have been due to the fact there was a rumor going around that chocolates were being served. And Bessie's chocolates didn't have the best reputation with the locals.

After poor Bessie's demise, I was informed by her lawyer that she had included me in her will, and I was the lucky recipient of all her chocolate recipes.

I picked them up and took them home and set the box on the counter, touched by Bessie's kind gesture. As I stared at the index cards with Bessie's scribbling all over them, I felt in my heart that I needed to find some way to prove to everyone that poor Bessie really was a world-class chocolatier. Okay, her kitchen did have a few sanitary issues, but I really did love the taste of her chocolates. It became my mission to show the town that she did have at least one winning recipe to die for. Scratch that. You know what I mean.

My perfect opportunity arose when the Sea Coast Mission, which holds a yearly chili cook-off fund-raiser for the Bar Harbor Food Pantry, decided to forgo chili in favor of chocolate in honor of Bessie. (This is a very forgiving town.)

Finally here was my chance! I searched through Bessie's chocolate recipes, hoping to find the perfect one; and about halfway through the stack, I found the one I was looking for. It was a recipe called "Hayley's Kisses," one Bessie created just for me. I knew for a fact they were delicious, because I ate almost the whole box in one sitting!

On the night of the chocolate fund-raiser, there were over thirty entries, and I swear half the town packed the mission to see who was going to win.

I walked around, nervously sampling bites of the competing chocolates, which had all been given a number so no one would know who baked which chocolates. Despite the stiff competition, I was still holding out hope for an upset.

When the big moment arrived, Mr. Ward, the head of the Sea Coast Mission, began announcing the winners, starting with third place. Number 16, Candy Appleton. Okay, yeah, her peanut butter cups weren't bad. Second place to number 9. Okay, Jeff Bingham's fudge brownies would make anyone swoon, but mostly because he adds a healthy dose of pot. Finally first place went to—drumroll, please—number 25. Me! It was me! I let out a whoop and raced to the front, and Mr. Ward handed me my grand prize, ten free movie tickets to Reel Pizza. He asked me what I called my winning chocolate recipe.

I smiled and turned to the audience and thanked everyone who chose my chocolates, and I told Mr. Ward they were called "Bessie's Bonbons," since it was she who had gifted me with the recipe. Everyone gasped in surprise. But then they began clapping for Bessie's now prize-winning chocolates. Well, everyone except for the Shop 'n Save owner Ron Hopkins, who had just taken a bite of my chocolates and then spit it out in his napkin and inspected it for cat hair.

It was a fitting tribute to Bessie's talent, and today I've already received five calls from friends asking for Bessie's special chocolate recipe. I know she's looking down from above, proud of the recognition she so richly deserves, and happy to share her recipe with the world. So here it is. But before you start baking, unwind with a soothing cocktail, like Bessie and I always loved to do.

Long-Day Bourbon Cocktail

<u>Ingredients</u>
2 clementine wedges
2 lemon wedges
2 ounces favorite bourbon
½ ounce Cointreau orange liqueur
2 dashes chocolate bitters

Muddle your orange and lemon in a cocktail shaker; then add all of your ingredients and add ice. Shake and strain into a cocktail glass. Grab a couple of bonbons and relax after a long day.

Bessie's First-Prize-Winning Bonbons

<u>Ingredients</u>
4 cups confectioners' sugar
1 cup ground pecans
½ cup plus 2 tablespoons sweetened condensed milk
¼ cup butter, softened
3 cups (18) ounces semisweet chocolate chips
2 tablespoons shortening

In a large bowl, combine your confectioners' sugar, pecans, milk, and butter. Roll into one-inch balls. Place on a waxed-paper-lined baking sheet. Cover and refrigerate overnight.

In a microwave melt your chocolate chips and shortening; stir until smooth. Dip the balls in the chocolate; allow excess to drip off. Place on waxed paper; let stand until set.

Index of Recipes

Please turn the page for an exciting sneak peek of

the next Hayley Powell mystery

DEATH OF A CHRISTMAS CATERER

coming soon from Kensington Publishing!

Chapter 1

"I friggin' hate Christmas!"

"You don't mean that," Hayley said, gripping her four oversized shopping bags while racing to catch up with Mona, who was veering toward the crowded food court at the Bangor Mall.

"Yes, I damn well do!" Mona barked as she plowed through a family of four that failed to get out of her way fast enough. She made a beeline for Sbarro's pizza and slapped her hand down on the counter causing the pimply faced kid behind the register to jump. "Pepperoni slice! Scratch that. Make it a whole pie!"

"Thanks, Mona, but I'm not really that hungry," Hayley said.

"Good. Because I wasn't offering. If I'm going to get through this day I'm going to need a large pizza and a pitcher of beer. I am so sick and tired

of these annoying holiday crowds swarming
around here like rats on a sinking ship!"

Hayley noticed a curly blond-haired little cherub
around six years old in an adorable reindeer
jumper listening to Mona and clutching her
mother's coat tighter. "Mona, lower your voice.
You're scaring children."

"Kids are the worst! Snot-nosed screaming
brats! You know Christmas would be so much
better if it was adults only. Just some spiked egg
nog, a warm fire, and a *Duck Dynasty* marathon on
TV. Heaven!"

Mona suddenly noticed the pimply Sbarro employee in his creased paper hat just staring at her.
"What? Do I have to come back there and kneed
the dough myself? Hop to it! I'm starving!"

The kid nodded, turning quickly and accidentally knocking over a stack of paper cups because he was so nervous dealing with an unstable
customer.

"And no husband!" Mona barked. "He's more
whiny and needy than my boatload of kids. Honestly, Hayley, just one year I'd like to spend the
holidays putting my feet up and relaxing instead
of brawling with some sumo-wrestling super mom
who wants the last Power Wheels Barbie Jammin'
Jeep for her spoiled rotten spawn!"

"You really do paint a picture, Mona."

Mona eyed the pimply kid, whose hand shook

as he ladled tomato sauce onto the pizza dough and splashed it around before slipping on a plastic glove and dunking his hand into a vat of mozzarella cheese.

Hayley rummaged in her coat pocket and pulled out a slip of paper, and began preusing it. "Look at how much stuff I still have to buy. I knew we should have gotten our Christmas shopping done right after Halloween. I never learn. Every year I plan on going early to avoid the crowds on Black Friday. And then I never get around to it and then I have to go on Black Friday, but this year I had the flu the entire Thanksgiving weekend and now I'm way behind on everything."

"Don't get so worked up, Hayley. You need to chill," Mona said.

Hayley glanced at Mona, mouth agape, but she missed it. She was too busy pounding her fist on the counter and yelling at Sbarro Boy. "Did you go to Italy to pick up the pepperoni? How long does it take to get a pie in the oven?"

"Mona, if you don't stop shouting at the poor boy, he's going to have a nervous breakdown."

Mona groaned and turned to the frightened teenager.

"Sorry, kid, I'm like a growling bear when I'm hungry," she said, slapping a twenty dollar bill down on the counter. "This is yours if I'm chowing down my pizza in the next ten minutes."

Sbarro Boy had that pie in the oven in nineteen seconds and was now grinning from ear to ear.

Hayley studied her list. "Gemma wants an iPad mini and Rhianna concert tickets. Dustin wants one, two, three . . . six video games for his X Box. There's no way I can afford all this."

Mona dipped into her coat pocket and pulled out a pen and thrust it in Hayley's face.

"What's that for?"

"Start crossing stuff off. Seriously. Why put yourself through this? Your kids will appreciate whatever you can afford to give them."

"You're right. I don't know why I feel the need to go overboard every year."

Hayley's cell phone chirped. She pulled it out of the back of her jeans and looked at the caller ID. "Oh, God. It's Danny."

"Don't pick up," Mona warned.

"I have to. The kids are going to go visit him for February vacation and I sent him their flight info this morning before we left for Bangor. He just needs to sign off and pay me back half the cost."

Danny Powell was Hayley's ex-husband who moved to Iowa after they divorced and was now living with a girl half his age named Becky.

Enough said.

"I swear, every time you talk to him, Hayley, he makes you feel bad. Just e-mail him when you get home."

"Maybe he can help me with the kids' wish list.

You know, we could split it up and he can buy some of these things they want."

"Have you *met* your ex-husband? Now you're just hoping for a friggin' Christmas miracle."

Hayley smiled and clicked on her phone. "Hi, Danny."

"Hey. Listen, this isn't going to work for me."

"What?"

"These tickets you bought for the kids to come see me during their February break. Three hundred a piece? What were you thinking?"

"They were the cheapest I could find."

"That's because you have them flying out on a Saturday. Weekends are always more expensive to travel."

"I couldn't book them for a Friday because I work, Danny. I'm out of vacation days and I can't afford to take any time off right now."

"How is that *my* problem?"

Unbelievable.

Hayley took a deep breath. "I understand how pricey it is. I was barely able to scrape together my half, Danny."

"It's too expensive. I can't pay you right now."

"I thought you were working extra shifts at Walmart during the holiday season."

"Yeah. But I got bills to pay, Hayley. You know how much it costs to heat our house in Des Moines during the winter?"

"No, I don't, Danny. Because it's just fun in the sun here in Maine!"

Hayley heard girlish giggling on the other end of the phone. "Who's that?"

"That's just Becky. We're having a little Christmas party here for a few friends and she got into the holiday punch a little early. Happy hour somewhere in the world, right?"

"Merry Christmas, Hayley," she heard Becky sing before erupting into a fit of giggles.

"Tell her I said 'Merry Christmas' back," Hayely sighed.

"Are you talking to the girlfriend?" Mona asked.

Hayley nodded.

"Hey, Danny, what'd you get Becky for Christmas this year? A Disney Crown Princess Tea Set?" Mona yelled before snorting at her own joke.

Hayley quickly covered the phone with her hand. "He can hear you."

"Good. Mission accomplished," Mona said, laughing.

"Is that Mona?" Danny said.

Hayley could picture her ex scowling. He never liked Mona. Mostly because she always despised him and never wanted Hayley to date him much less marry him.

If Hayley had only listened to Mona in high school.

But then again, he did help her bring two of the most amazing kids into the world.

Just one mother's opinion.

"Well, you tell her I'm taking Becky to Bermuda for Christmas!" Danny shouted. "That's right! We'll be lounging by the pool while she's trying on that pair of itchy gray wool socks her deadbeat husband buys her every year."

"Wait. What? I thought you just said you were broke."

There was a long uneasy silence.

"Danny? Are you still there?"

"Yeah, I'm here."

"You're going to Bermuda?"

"Now don't jump down my throat. We got a good deal. And I bought the package before I knew how much the kids' plane tickets were going to cost."

"That's why you can't pay me back?"

The only place Danny ever took Hayley when they were married was a campground in Moosehead Lake one weekend. And then they had to leave early because it rained the whole time and a Maine black bear ate all of their supplies while they went into town to buy umbrellas and a box of wine.

Hayley didn't want to engage Danny anymore than she already had. She took another deep breath and calmly held the phone to her ear.

"Okay. I'm sure you'll pay me back just as soon as you can."

"Absolutely. There's a girl at work who is about to drop a baby after New Year's and she's promised to give me some of her shifts while she's out on maternity leave so I can make some extra cash."

"Fine. Now would you do me a favor? Dustin really wants this new Metal Gear video game that just came out and I was hoping you might be able to . . ."

"No. I told you, Hayley. I'm broke."

"It's under thirty dollars."

"No can do. Sorry."

"What? Did you spend your last twenty bucks on a new thong for Becky?"

She just couldn't resist.

"You really should stop spoiling the kids, Hayley," Danny said.

"Please. Not this again."

"You do this every year. Every December around this time your bank account is empty and yet you just can't help yourself. You max out your last working credit card buying all this junk the kids don't need just so they have a nice Christmas. And we both know why."

"I don't need a lecture from you, Danny."

"You overcompensate because you feel guilty."

"Somebody's been watching Dr. Phil again."

"It's true. You divorced me and now the kids are the victims of a broken home and you can't live with yourself so you go all out to make up for it during the holidays just to alleviate some of the guilt."

"Alleviate? I didn't know you played *Words with Friends*."

"You can make fun of me all you want. We both know I'm right."

"Have fun in Bermuda," Hayley said, ending the call.

She turned to Mona.

"Come on, Mona. Let's go. We have some serious shopping to do."

"Don't let him get to you, Hayley."

Hayley fished a Visa card out of her bag. "I think this one may have some credit left on it."

"You're going to regret this, Hayley."

"Gemma needs some new ski boots. Let's start at Dillard's."

"What about my pizza?"

"Get it to go."

Mona knew there was no point in arguing.

Hayley was on a mission.

She knew when she was driving home to Bar Harbor in Mona's truck, the flatbed filled with shopping bags, she would realize Mona was absolutely right. That she once again allowed her ex-husband to get under her skin because she knew on some level he was right, and she just played into his hand by spending far too much money on the kids.

Was it so wrong to want a Merry Christmas for her kids?

She would just pray that there was no expensive emergency between now and the time Sal doled out her year-end Christmas bonus at the *Island Times* where she worked.

But unbeknownst to Hayley there was indeed going to be an emergency.

A really big one.

And it wasn't going to involve a threatening phone call from a creditor.

No. This emergency was going to involve a dead body.

GREAT BOOKS,
GREAT SAVINGS!

When You Visit Our Website:
www.kensingtonbooks.com
You Can Save Money Off The Retail Price
Of Any Book You Purchase!

- • All Your Favorite Kensington Authors
- • New Releases & Timeless Classics
- • Overnight Shipping Available
- • eBooks Available For Many Titles
- • All Major Credit Cards Accepted

Visit Us Today To Start Saving!
www.kensingtonbooks.com

All Orders Are Subject To Availability.
Shipping and Handling Charges Apply.
Offers and Prices Subject To Change Without Notice.